ENCOUNTER

▶ ▶ ▶ ▶ ▶ ▶ ▶ ▶ ▶ ▶

Standing right outside the window—actually, hovering at about twenty yards off the deck—was a bright blue oval light about twelve feet in diameter. Another stood slightly above and several hundred yards to the rear, and it was much larger. It is very difficult to describe these things because the colors are unlike any color we usually experience on earth, and the movements are unlike anything we usually see moving through our skies. Even the light itself has a different quality, otherworldly, totally alien.

The small saucer was doing a little dance.

Just sort of a graceful wobble, tilting on its axis in a rhythmic dance.

And Julie's body was sort of duplicating that motion.

The implications were fairly obvious.

They were conversing.

TIME
TO
TIME

**THE ASHTON FORD NOVELS
by Don Pendleton**

Ashes to Ashes
Eye to Eye
Mind to Mind
Life to Life
Heart to Heart
Time to Time

**PUBLISHED BY
POPULAR LIBRARY**

ATTENTION: SCHOOLS AND CORPORATIONS

POPULAR LIBRARY books are available at quantity discounts with bulk purchase for educational, business, or sales promotional use. For information, please write to SPECIAL SALES DEPARTMENT, POPULAR LIBRARY, 666 FIFTH AVENUE, NEW YORK, N Y 10103

**ARE THERE POPULAR LIBRARY BOOKS
YOU WANT BUT CANNOT FIND IN YOUR LOCAL STORES?**

You can get any POPULAR LIBRARY title in print. Simply send title and retail price, plus 50¢ per order and 50¢ per copy to cover mailing and handling costs for each book desired. New York State and California residents add applicable sales tax. Enclose check or money order only, no cash please, to POPULAR LIBRARY, P. O. BOX 690, NEW YORK, N Y 10019

DON PENDLETON

TIME TO TIME

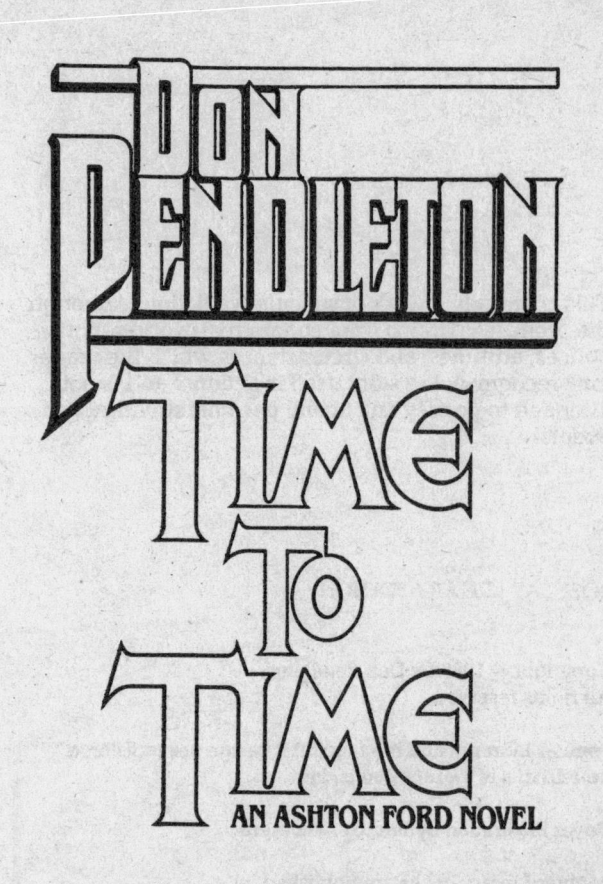

AN ASHTON FORD NOVEL

POPULAR LIBRARY

An Imprint of Warner Books, Inc.

A Warner Communications Company

This is entirely a work of speculative fiction. Although the premise is drawn from certain real-world reports, notices, attitudes, and circumstances which the reader may recognize, the story itself is fictional and is not intended to portray any actual persons, situations, or events.

POPULAR LIBRARY EDITION

Copyright © 1988 by Don Pendleton
All rights reserved.

Popular Library® and the fanciful P design are registered trademarks of Warner Books, Inc.

Cover illustration by Franco Accornero

Popular Library books are published by
Warner Books, Inc.
666 Fifth Avenue
New York, N.Y. 10103

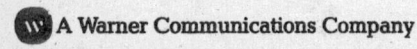

A Warner Communications Company

Printed in the United States of America

First Printing: March, 1988

10 9 8 7 6 5 4 3 2 1

For all those who have shared the experience, and still wonder. Take peace.

                                                dp

Author's Note

To My Readers:

Ashton Ford will come as something of a surprise to those of you who have been with me over the years. This is not the same type of fiction that established my success as a novelist; Ford is not a gutbuster and he is not trying to save the world from anything but its own confusion. There are no grenade launchers or rockets to solve his problems and he is more of a lover than a fighter.

Some have wondered why I was silent for so many years; some will now also wonder why I have returned in such altered form. The truth is that I had said all I had to say about that other aspect of life. I have grown, I hope, both as a person and as a writer, and I needed another vehicle to carry the creative quest. Ashton Ford is that vehicle. Through this character I attempt to understand more fully and to give better meaning to my perceptions of what is going on here on Planet Earth, and the greatest mystery of all the mysteries: the *why* of existence itself.

Through Ford I use everything I can reach in

the total knowledge of mankind to elaborate this mystery and to arm my characters for the quest. I try to entertain myself with their adventures, hoping that what entertains me may also entertain others—so these books, like life itself, are not all grim purpose and trembling truths. They are fun to write; for some they will be fun to read. To each of those I dedicate the work, and I solicit their response. Please let me hear from you, care of Warner Books, 666 Fifth Avenue, New York, NY 10103. My warm best wishes to you all,

Don Pendleton

CHAPTER ONE

Once Upon a Time

How do you feel about flying saucers? I always wanted to see one. Wanted to ride in one. I kept hearing the same stories you've heard—read all the books, watched all the movies, even spent time camped on a hillside during several "flap" periods. Never caught even a glimpse of one. Was never contacted or confronted or approached in any way by visitors from another star.

Or so I thought, anyway.

Turns out I could've been wrong about that for quite a long time.

You could be wrong, too, if you think you've never been contacted.

The sensing I get now is that quite a number of people on this planet could be intimately involved with other-star beings without consciously realizing it. The stories that get written about and talked about could represent nothing more than a few odd incidents here and there that somehow misfired or went wrong.

1

I get another sensing that all of us may be aliens, too. Alien to this planet, I mean. All of human life. Maybe it did not start here. Or if it did start here, maybe it was started deliberately by some of those daring beings in their flying machines who needed biological robots to assist them in their work with this planet.

I have evidence to back up these sensings.

That is what this case is about. So be forewarned. If you believe that UFO phenomena can all be explained in purely psychological terms, then you may not enjoy this case as I did; maybe you should just take a walk right now. Or maybe you shouldn't. I have evidence also to suggest that the most hard-nosed skeptics may unwittingly be the most involved in all this intrigue.

Whatever your cast of mind, I have no interest here in changing it. I just have a very interesting story to tell you, and you can make up your own mind as to what it means to you. I *hope* you can make up your own mind. I'm not too sure about that either anymore, for any of us on this planet.

Once upon a time, you see, long, long ago—about, I figure, eight hundred million years ago...

CHAPTER TWO
At First Sight

Ted Bransen was waiting in his Bentley outside my Malibu beach pad when I returned home one night recently. I had been to one of those celebrity soirees in Beverly Hills and I'd seen him there, although we had not spoken. I thought I'd left early so I was more than a little surprised to find the guy at my front door.

Ted is a pretty good doubles partner and he also has a backhand that comes right off the ground, but that is about the best I can say for him. I never spent a lot of time with him off the court. He'd never seemed to seek my company either, which is another reason why I was surprised to find him waiting for me.

I don't know his age but he's pushing forty and his miles are beginning to show. Still a very handsome guy if you're going just for surface, and he can be pienty charming when he wants to be. He can also be nasty as hell and I think he has more enemies than friends in the community. In fact, I would probably have to say that most of his friends come via his wife. He is married to Penny Laker. Yeah, *that* Penny Laker.

The guy never made much for himself in pictures but he did the next best thing, married Penny and took over the management of her career, which—to his credit—has been going nowhere but up ever since.

So I was wondering why the guy was parked outside my house at Malibu in the middle of the night when we'd been in the same room together without speaking an hour or so earlier.

I went on past him and tucked my Maserati in the garage, then came back through the house to see if he was still there. He was, nervously working at a cigarette and staring at my door. So I went back out and spoke to him through the open window of his Bentley.

"Lose something, Ted?"

"No, I was just waiting to see if someone might be following you home."

"*Some*one?"

He blew smoke at me and replied, "No one in particular. Take it easy. This is no jealous husband routine."

Well, I was glad to hear that—though I hadn't really thought of that scenario myself.

"Just didn't want to crowd the court for you, in case, ahhh..."

I said, "Saw you at Chasen's."

He said, "Saw you too. That's what—uh, meant to speak to you. Time I got around to it, you were gone. So I..."

"Beat me home," I observed.

He grinned. "In that Maserati? You must have stopped along the way."

Matter of fact, I had.

I said, "You didn't come all the way up here just to say hello."

"'Course not."

I sighed. "Well, come inside and I'll rassle us up a pot of coffee."

"I really don't have time for that, Ash," he replied. "But I want to retain you. Can we get together tomorrow and discuss it?"

"Retain me for what?"

His eyes twitched as he told me, "Penny's into some kind of weird shit and it's driving me crazy. I'd rather not get into the details right now because I really need to get back into town, but let's—"

"Why didn't you just call me?"

"Look, this has to be absolutely confidential. I'm even afraid to use the telephone. And I couldn't really approach you at the party, could I, with all those columnists nosing around with their micro-recorders humming away. Look, I'll be honest, I didn't even think of you until I saw you tonight. Then it hit me. Shit!—*there's* the guy for the job!"

"What job?" I inquired quietly.

"She's into this weird..."

"My kind of weird, huh."

"Think so, yeah. Only maybe worse. I mean, this isn't tea leaves and birth signs. It's something very heavy. And it's going to wreck her career if I can't get her out of it."

I commented, "She's past twenty-one, Ted. What do you expect me to do?"

"Let's discuss it tomorrow."

"Can't," I lied. "I'm tied up the rest of the week—rest of the month, in fact. Sorry."

He reached through the car window and put a hand on my arm, snarling, "Cut that shit! This is Ted! I'm coming to you for help!"

"For Penny."

"Of course for Penny."

I happened to like Penny Laker quite a lot. Not that we are old friends or even new friends, but we do move about in the same circles and there have been occasional opportunities for quiet conversations. I get invited to a lot of the happenings in town. Not that I am one of them but more like, I think, a part of the atmosphere. I'm a conversation piece, you see. This is Ashton Ford. He's a psychic. He solves crimes. He can tell your future. Ask him about your career. (That's always a big one, in this town.) Ask him how to improve your sex life. (So's that one.) Ask him about cosmic sex. (Double bingo.)

Don't wonder why I put up with that. The truth is that often I enjoy it. I'm human. And it sure as hell improves *my* sex life.

But Penny Laker had never asked me to teach her cosmic sex, had never inquired about her career, and always seemed too engrossed in the present moment even to wonder about the future.

Fascination, I guess, is the word. The lady had a fascination for the life processes—and when we talked, we talked *deep*.

I liked her.

So I told her prick of a husband: "Tell Penny to give me a call."

The prick told me, "You can't be that dumb! You know

Penny! She'd have a *fit* if she thought I was interfering with..."

"With what?"

"With this new craziness! How the hell do I know what it is? Last year it was trance-channeling, then it was the interdimensional whatever harmonic convergence, then it was—listen!—she hasn't worked for six months, won't look at a script, won't take calls from her agent! I'm crazy with this! I think she's goddamn getting menopausal fits or something."

Not unless she had awfully good plastic surgeons.

I said quietly, "She couldn't be more than thirty-five."

He growled, "You're a decade short, Ford."

I was just playing at this point. I told him, "Then maybe you should be talking to her gynecologist."

He said, "She doesn't *have* a gynecologist. Doesn't have a family physician. Uses herbal remedies and meditation. How the hell do I consult her spirit guides? Look, she's in trouble. She needs help. I'm crazy with it."

I thought, Well, maybe he is.

Just because *I* never liked the guy didn't mean...

I told him, "Okay. Your place or mine?"

He quickly replied, "Neutral ground. Meet me at the Polo Lounge at noon sharp. I'll have a table."

I agreed to that.

He cranked the engine and drove away.

I was standing at the curb and watching that departure with a curious feeling of total detachment when I became aware of a low-pitched humming sound that seemed to be coming from the darkness above the house.

I swiveled about for a look just as a luminously glowing disc tilted up over the rooftop and moved smoothly away in apparent pursuit of the departing car. I guess my mind just sort of froze on that sight.

The thing was about twelve feet in diameter and very thin except for a little housing on top, and it really was not there long enough for me to shift into objective mode and look for details.

I just stood there gawking until car and disc disappeared into the darkness.

Funny. I'd never really expected to see one. I still was not sure that I had.

But I knew for damn sure that it was going to seem a long wait for that noon meeting in the Polo Lounge.

CHAPTER THREE

A Problem in Graphics

I just could not get to sleep. My eyes felt strained and strange but when I closed them, I would get this flood of brilliantly colored images, mostly geometric shapes in a slow tumbling motion almost like computer graphics displaying three-dimensional images and slowly turning them this way and that for different perspectives but always looking the same whatever the perspective.

I fought that for about twenty minutes, then gave it up and slipped into a robe, lit a cigarette, stepped out onto the deck, and stared at the phosphorescent surf for a few minutes. It did not help a hell of a lot. The eyes were still faintly burning and my vision slightly blurred when I went back inside—and now, on top of it, I was getting these slowly tumbling golden triangles superimposed over my open-eyed vision.

I put on a pot of coffee and made an effort to understand what was happening. Mental imagery is no new thing for me, not even involuntary imagery. But this was different, and a lot more persistent than the stuff I'd become accustomed to. This is right-brain stuff, you know. The nonverbal side of the mind. That is where the emotions live, where creativity lurks, where inspiration and intuition do their thing. Being nonverbal, it deals entirely with graphics.

I'd been doing a lot of thinking lately as to whether the right brain creates the graphics or if it merely acts as a receiver for graphics that are generated elsewhere. You can make "elsewhere" whatever you'd like.

Carl Jung hypothesized a collective unconscious that communicates with mankind via a system of universal symbology. I have a good friend who is a highly successful psychiatrist and also happens to be somewhat psychic. He seems to have settled around a theory that the collective unconscious is actually that psychic faculty present in all humans as a natural function of the right brain. In other words, the whole human race is linked together sort of like a single huge organism, with that linkage through the right brain. Which is his way of explaining extrasensory perception. He thinks that everyone's right brain is continually trying to influence the intellectual centers on the left side, but that humanity long ago began relying more on the left brain than the right, and that is why we have developed intellectually much more rapidly than we have developed spiritually.

I'd been giving some thought to that idea. Actually it could explain a lot more than mere ESP; carried to the logical inferences, it would maybe explain the constant inner conflict experienced by most people and the whole array of mental illnesses that afflict the human race. It would be like *every*one has a split personality—split right down the middle between left and right hemispheres, with the two as virtual strangers because they speak different languages.

Most all of the mystics complain of this curious dichotomy within the human framework. St. Paul wrote lyrically of the problem: "For the flesh lusteth against the Spirit, and the Spirit against the flesh; and these are contrary the one to the other: so that ye cannot do the things that ye would" (Galatians 5:17). Remove that statement from its religious context and you're talking modern psychiatry.

I guess psychiatry was on my mind that night because I was wondering if I could trust my own mental impressions. *Seeing* is a mental impression, you know. Had I actually seen the thing?

If so—or even if not—what was I seeing now—and why was I seeing it?

I had done some UFO research. And I knew that a respectable body of scientific thought on the question was regarding the entire thing as purely mental phenomena. Jung's damned symbols, I supposed. Which was not to say that the UFOs were not *real;* just not real in the physical sense. Constructs of the mind—of the collective planetary mind—but very real, as such.

Well, it was two o'clock and I was still thinking like that and trying to fend off the slow-motion graphics that kept tumbling out of my head. I'd drunk the whole pot of coffee and stubbed out far too many cigarettes. But I knew it would be useless to try to take that stuff back to bed, so I showered and shaved and got dressed, rolled the Maserati out, and drove up into the hills.

Don't ask why I went that way. I don't know why I

went that way. It is sheer wilderness up there. There was nothing up there I'd lost or was looking for. I thought.

But I damn near ran down Penny Laker.

She was stumbling along the highway up there above Pepperdine and she was stark naked. I didn't know it was her at first, not until she looked over her shoulder into my headlights. Then I had to chase her down on foot because she started running as for her life. I grabbed her and had to fight her all the way back to the car. She wasn't screaming, just grunting in total panic and thrashing like hell with all four limbs.

I don't know at what point in all that my own mind stopped its graphic tumbling, nor do I know with any precision how I got Penny into the car and calmed down enough to drive her away from there. I do know that I saw a shooting star move directly across our path as we were descending the mountain, then another a moment later, moving in the opposite direction. At that point, I know, my graphics had turned off.

I took off my shirt and wrapped Penny in it, then I took her to my place.

She was a basket case, mentally. Didn't seem to know where she was or who I was or even who she was. She'd become entirely docile, doing whatever I suggested without argument or resistance of any kind.

I took her in the house and put her to bed, inspected her for physical hurts and found none. She was asleep before I could get her tucked in good.

I went straight to the telephone and called Ted Bransen. He answered the second ring with a sleepy voice that turned a bit nasty when I asked him if he knew where his wife was.

He snarled, "I *told* you, dammit, that you're working this through *me!*"

I was too drained and confused to snarl back. I just replied in a very meek voice, "Call me if you are curious about her," and hung up.

He called back about twenty seconds later and yelled, "She's not in her bed! Do you know where she is?"

"She's in my bed, pal," I told him, and hung up again. This time I turned off the ringer.

It was, I figured, about a twenty-minute drive at that time of night from his house to mine.

Meanwhile I was tired as hell and fading fast. I felt curiously lethargic, drained, spent. I don't get that way often, no matter how long the night.

So I went to the bar and splashed some bourbon onto an ice cube, took it to the picture window overlooking the Pacific.

It was damned pretty out there, star-spangled above and phosphorescent below, just enough wind to make some caps atop the surging waters.

Gradually I became aware that there was just a bit too much glow out there. I'd looked out that window often enough in all kinds of weather to recognize a different quality to this night.

The glow continued growing until finally it was suspended right out there in front of me along the water line. It was oval-shaped and about twelve feet across. I swear the damned thing waved at me; it sort of wobbled in the air, like a bowl bouncing around when you set it down too hard. And then, maybe just to show me where my graphics had originated, it sent me another golden triangle tumbling gently through my head.

Then, instantly, *it* became an identical golden triangle, slowly inverted itself with the point skyward, and shot straight up without a sound.

I was still staring at the place where it had been when another "shooting star" whizzed across the horizon, far at sea.

Some things the thinking mind simply refuses to process. Mine was definitely beginning to balk at the whole thing.

Take away the saucer, even, and there is too much to process.

I took my bourbon onto the open deck and stretched out with it on a chaise, allowing my eyes to find their own way into those star-spangled depths suspended above my head.

Nothing was real; that was my illumination of the moment.

All was illusion.

But still I was wondering what the hell I'd gotten myself into this time.

CHAPTER FOUR

Etchings

Either Penny Laker is a master at disinformation or someone around her is. Published background information on this superstar is a beautiful study in contradictions. She has been variously reported as a native of Illinois, Scotland, Ireland, Australia, Canada, and Iceland. Depending upon where she was born, her age might be somewhere between thirty-three and thirty-nine. She got her start as an actress either on Broadway, at Burt Reynolds's theater in Florida, on the London stage, in an Italian movie, or in San Francisco in a porno film.

She appeared on the Hollywood scene ten years ago with a supporting role in a much ballyhooed picture that was a box-office flop but nevertheless launched Penny Laker with rave reviews, comparing her with the best in the business. She has been one of the "hot properties" in a highly property-conscious town ever since, but that is not the end of disinformation. Perhaps one of the most written-about stars in the modern era, no two stories agree as to the details of that mercurial career.

It *appears* that she met Ted Bransen during her third year in Hollywood—but that's not certain—and they were married either in Mexico City or Monte Carlo or Zurich, take your pick. It was the first or third marriage for both, and Penny has either two or three grown kids somewhere in Europe or South America.

I call all that not sloppy reporting but disinformation. Someone was doing this on purpose, to a calculated effect.

I am not exactly a babe in the woods in such matters. I am not really a detective and I may not even really be psychic (because I still don't know what "psychic" is) but I do have a pretty good grounding in the informational sciences and I held down a desk in the Pentagon at the Office of Naval Intelligence for several years. My family name is not really Ford but I am an Ashton via my mother. Nobody but Mother ever knew who my father was, and I'm not sure that she knew—but she told me once in a moment of candid humor that I was a "son of the Ford," which is navy talk from a family with all its proudest moments in naval service.

One of my ancestors was politically influential in the selection of Annapolis as the site of the U.S. Naval Academy, but the naval heritage goes even beyond that. Anyway, "son of a gun" is an old naval term denoting an illegitimate child, and it stems from the early days when civilian women served domestically on vessels of war. Since the guns were always emplaced at the vessel's center of gravity, it was beneath these guns that such women crawled to deliver their misbegotten offspring;

thus, children of questionable paternity were referred to as "son of the gun."

I know that I was not born in my mother's Ford Fairlane so she was undoubtedly referring to my conception therein. It was either an item of delicious memory or ironic humor that the name on my birth certificate is Ford. Don't ask why I was not properly given my legal name, Ashton, at the rear instead of at the front; Mother was sensitive about that and always managed to change the subject when I brought it up. Maybe there was a problem with my grandparents. I wouldn't know; I never met them. My mother never married and I was raised in the Ashton naval tradition, hence Annapolis and the obligated service that followed.

I give you all that just so you know where I'm coming from when I tell you that it appeared to me that the real Penny Laker was very well concealed behind an entirely effective disinformational cover. It is easier for women than men to get away with something like that because few women die with the name they were born to, and there is traditionally less legal identification of women as they move through life.

I was thinking about all that, of course, as I waited for Ted Bransen to come claim his naked wife from my bed. And I do not mind admitting that I was feeling a bit defensive about that confrontation with Bransen. He can be a real jerk. And I did not have a really coherent story to give the guy. So how do I explain Penny Laker naked in my bed to her jerk of a husband?

As it turned out, it was a needless worry.

Ted Bransen did not come for his wife. He sent another. *Quite* another. She introduced herself as Julie Marsini and told me that she was Penny's personal secretary. I could buy it because I'd seen her before and wondered about her before. I'd also seen her workout suit, or one like it, in a shop window on Rodeo Drive; she looked like she'd just come from Jane Fonda's body salon or some such. Think of understated beauty, a woman who takes no obvious pains either to enhance or conceal the natural endowments—almost like one of the gray people who are always around yet hardly noticeable—young but not too young, pretty but not dramatically pretty, well built but not seductively displayed, interesting but not overpoweringly so. She had absolutely raven-black hair, worn neatly at less than shoulder length, and the darkest eyes I'd ever seen set into such fair skin. Beautiful mouth. Nice hands—expressive, without exaggerated movements—delicate and artful but also entirely capable. A soft fabric handbag with a silkrope draw was slung casually from one shoulder.

I also liked her no-nonsense manner, which still managed to be conveyed graciously.

"Thank you for calling, Mr. Ford. May I see her now?"

"Wait a minute," I said. Guess I was still hung up on my Ted Bransen defenses. "Don't you want to know why she's here?"

"If that is important, I'm sure she'll tell me. She *is* all right?"

I rubbed my temple as I replied, "Far as I can tell, physically, yeah, she's fine. But she was totally disoriented when I found her, and we've had absolutely no conversation. Sleeping like a baby for the past hour."

"Then maybe we shouldn't disturb her." That voice fit

the rest of her—understated strength, properly concerned, but unemotional, coolly modulated.

I said, "She's, uh, in my bed. It's the only bed in the house." I glanced at my watch. "It's three o'clock. I have a big day coming up."

My shrinking sense of hospitality gave her no pause. "Could you go to a hotel for the rest of the night? Of course we would cover your expenses."

I said, "No dice. My bed is not for rent. Speaking of which, why didn't Bransen come? Or has this sort of thing become too routine for him?"

She showed me a briefly disappointed look, then replied, "That could be highly confrontational, couldn't it? Why should he want to embarrass either of you?"

I shrugged and said, "Well, maybe I've misread the guy. I expected him to come in here breathing fire and screaming accusations."

She smiled, barely, as she told me, "I can understand your position. Rest assured that there are no suspicions of . . . romantic indiscretion."

I asked her, "Do you always talk like that?"

"Like what?"

"The perfect executive secretary."

She laughed lightly, said, "Thank you," and broke eye contact.

I showed her to the bedroom. I'd left a small bedside lamp on and the lighting in there was sort of mellow. Penny was lying just as I'd left her—flat on her back, head straight on the pillow—but she looked different somehow, almost ghastly pale in the muted light. Totally still, no signs of breathing, she looked like a corpse.

I had halted just inside the bedroom door. Julie went on

to the foot of the bed and spoke a single word so softly that I could not be sure what it was, but I assumed she'd called Penny's name because she responded immediately in an equally soft voice, though without opening her eyes.

Julie turned to me and said, "We'll be right out."

I suddenly felt like an ass. I told her, "Hey, I can sleep on the couch if..."

"No, no," she replied, "it will be fine now. Just give us a minute please."

"She lost her clothes somewhere," I said.

"No problem."

No problem, okay. But can you understand how very strange I was feeling about all this? Forgetting the saucers, even—forget I even mentioned them—does the strangeness translate here? I had chanced upon a Hollywood superstar staggering naked along a deserted road in a remote area in the middle of the night. Other than that bare fact, there was no evidence of foul play or physical harm of any kind—except that the lady was confused and disoriented. So I take her to my home and put her to bed and call her husband, who a short time earlier had evinced a strong concern for her well-being.

So does the husband come tearing in to collect her naked body from my bed? Hell no. The lady's secretary comes, and then the whole thing is just cool business as usual with "no problem."

Well it was a hell of a problem for me.

I skulked around the kitchen for about ten minutes, expecting each moment to bring Julie back out with a semiconscious superstar staggering along beside her draped in a sheet or some such.

Instead I got two very lively and cheerful—not to mention beautiful—women dressed identically in workout suits. So I guess you can easily conceal one of those things in a woman's handbag, even the ballerina-style shoes.

Penny stretched up from her toes to plant a moist kiss on my chin. "Thank you, Ashton," she said in a perfectly normal voice, and with about the same emotion one would use to acknowledge a simple courtesy.

I muttered, "Don't mention it."

"I'll call you later."

"Please do that."

Julie gave me an enigmatic smile and they departed arm in arm.

I stepped outside and watched the car pull away, half expecting to get another look at a saucer.

In fact, I stood stock-still for fully two minutes *waiting* for the saucer. It did not show. Back inside, I saw no evidence of any of it. The bed was neatly made with no appearance of having been occupied that night.

I didn't know what the hell to think. But I must have been pretty heavily into it, because I realized with a start that I was standing at the big picture window onto the sea with no memory of walking in there. That's where I found the evidence. Not through the window but inside the window itself, in the glass, a peculiar etching or some such, about the size of my fist: a perfect triangle. It's still there. Come see it someday, if you'd like.

I did not need to look at it all that much.

The damn thing was already etched into my brain.

CHAPTER FIVE

First Star I See Tonight

I did not have lunch with Ted Bransen that day. His office awakened me with a nine o'clock call to cancel the appointment without explanation. Suited me fine. I had not gotten to sleep before dawn anyway, so I was in a welcome mood for a few more hours between the sheets.

Didn't work out that way, though. Couldn't go back to sleep, couldn't get any of it off my mind just lying there, so I got up a few minutes later and hit the shower. I usually listen to NewsRadio over breakfast via the kitchen radio because they give me the world every morning in capsule form, true to their claim, and because I've found that is about all the world I need on a daily basis.

So before I even got my coffee I learned that we'd had a full-blown UFO flap during the night, not just in the Los Angeles area but from Baja to the Golden Gate and points inland. That quivered the old antennae, let me tell you.

Apparently there'd been a hell of a concentration of

22

sightings in my immediate area, and an L.A. County sheriff's deputy had chased a saucer in his patrol car all the way through Malibu Canyon. I had found Penny Laker on the ocean side of that canyon, very close to the spot where the deputy first spotted his saucer, and the time frame was about right.

So I climbed on the telephone and began running the thing down. My friend Willie Wilson, who strings for AP, told me that the sheriff's office was trying to quieten the thing, but he also told me that a television crew had managed to sneak some tape on the patrol car involved, which had taken quite a beating during the chase. Apparently the vehicle had scraped the canyon wall a couple of times and finally ended up in a field at the north end with two flat tires and an hysterical officer yelling for help via the radio.

So I postponed breakfast and met Willie in downtown L.A. and we had coffee and doughnuts with the cameraman from the television unit. This guy's name is Joe White and he is black, has a very droll sense of humor, hugely enjoyed his latest assignment. He rolled his eyes at me over his coffee and said, "Hell, I've been telling 'em for years that there's something up there. I reported one myself some years back and I can still remember the way those cops were looking at me—you know, like wondering what my angle was or how much junk I'd been sniffing. Does me good to see they react to it the same way I did. That guy tore his damn car all to hell—I mean, practically totaled. Claims he kept losing power and couldn't steer. Shit. Let me tell you, nobody can steer with the eyes glued to the sky and the foot glued to the accelerator. I been through all that myself."

But I wanted the officer's name and Joe White did not want to give me that. "Man has been ridiculed enough," he declared quietly. "Leave 'im alone."

"I saw it, too, Joe," I told him, just as quietly. "I don't want to ridicule the man. Just want to talk to him."

"Did you file a report?"

"No."

"Don't. Let that be my advice from one who did. Don't."

I said, "I need to talk to the man, Joe."

"Won't do you no good," he said. "Anyway, he's in the hospital."

"County General?"

"Yeah." He smiled suddenly. "You really do have the itch, don't you."

"Where it can't be scratched, right."

Those expressive eyes rolled again. "You haven't talked to me."

"Right."

"Ask for Grover Dalton."

I thanked my media friends, picked up the check, and went straight to County General.

The man was under no wraps whatsoever. He shared a room with three other men and all four looked perfectly healthy to me. Except that Dalton's eyes were troubled and wary, kept flicking upward in an involuntary reflex. I sat on the edge of his bed with what I hoped was a professional manner and made a big thing of checking his eyes. I'd already checked his chart. He was on a mild antianxiety medication, nothing else.

"Feeling better now, Grover?"

"Yes, sir. When can I go home?"

"Soon. The quicker you get fully relaxed about all this, the quicker you'll be home."

"I'll never get relaxed about all this, sir, until people start believing me. I want a lie detector."

"I believe you, Grover."

"Do you?"

"Sure I do. Saw the damn thing myself, right close to where you saw it."

"Oh! Well! Did you tell...?"

"Not yet. But I will. About twelve-foot diameter, waffle-thin, with a dome on top, blue lights."

"That's it! That's what I saw! And underneath—when it comes up and floats over you—underneath there's these circular revolving lights, the little jets like blowtorches coming out the sides—did you see that?"

I said, "Well, I didn't keep with it the way you did. Led you a hell of a chase, didn't it."

"The damned thing was sucking me on. I can see that now. It was maneuvering through that canyon at no more than twenty feet off the ground. Didn't need to do that. Could've just gone up and over, 'cause when it did finally take off, it went straight up like a skyrocket and was clean out of sight before I could even think about it."

"That was when you were in the open field?"

"Yes, sir."

"What was it doing when you first saw it?"

"Well it just jumped across the road and started wiggling at me."

"Wiggling?"

"Yes, sir, like standing still in the air but bouncing side to side."

"I understand. Then what happened?"

"Well see, I was—there was this woman—I came around the bend and saw this woman in the middle of the road, had to slam my brakes to avoid her. And off to the side, off the road, I could see these eyes reflecting my headlights as I swerved around trying to avoid the woman—you know like deer's eyes reflect in the night? —only these were like big round bug eyes, I mean several pair of them, and I could see movement in the bushes, and..."

"What was the woman doing?"

"She was just standing there in the middle of the road."

"How was she dressed?"

"I don't—I believe she wasn't dressed, or not very. It all happened so quick—but I'm *sure* I saw a woman in the road, that's why I braked."

"And then?"

"Well I was... really thinking about the woman, I guess. But even before I got the car under control, this *thing* jumped up at me—like you described it, sir, that's the same thing I saw. And I saw these little figures scurrying around outside of it, and then it just leapt up about twenty feet off the ground and started dancing at me. I was—listen, I was scared to death and I don't mind saying so. But I feel like an ass now because..."

"Because what?"

"Well because I was going to the woman's aid. I mean that's what I had in mind, and it's what I should have done. But then the damn thing just lured me away from her."

"You're sure of that, huh."

"Thinking back on it, yes sir, I'm sure of that. It started off real slow, just dancing along. I jumped back in the patrol car and went after it. No matter how fast I went, it just hung out there about fifty feet ahead. All the way through the canyon like that. And my headlights kept going off and back on again, my engine was losing compression, and my radio was crazy with static even with the squelch all the way up. Kept losing the steering. Hell I wanted to stop but I *couldn't* stop, it was like I was hypnotized or something, I just kept right on after it even though that was the last thing in the world I wanted to do."

"You wanted out."

"Damn right I wanted out but they wouldn't let me out."

"They who?"

"They the bug-eyed bastards in the UFO. They finally dropped me in the middle of a field."

"*Dropped* you?"

"Yes, sir. My wheels weren't even on the ground the last mile or two."

"That's uh, pretty far-out, isn't it."

"I don't care how far-out it is. That's what happened."

Poor guy was getting all worked up. I patted his hand and left him sitting there with his eyes twitching, stopped at the nurse's station and again consulted his chart, handed the chart to the nurse with a meaningful look, and told her, "He's almost due for his medication. Better do it now."

She replied, "Yes, Doctor," with hardly a second look at me.

It was the psycho ward.

But at least one patient in there was as sane as anybody. The danger now, as I saw it, was that maybe he would not be sane for long. Close encounters have a way of jangling the mind. I had to wonder why that was so. Was there something buried in genetic memory, something terrifying and horrible, that was activated by these experiences?

I happened to know, because I'd been keeping on top of it, that a whole new school of medicine was arising around these unfortunate contactees—and I knew a man in Washington who was the unofficial dean of that school.

So I went to a phone booth right there at the hospital and gave him a call. "Is this about the California flap?" he immediately asked me.

"It is," I replied, and I told him about Grover Dalton. "Can you swing some help his way?"

"I can try," he said wearily.

He needed to try. Police officers are especially vulnerable to the UFO Depression Syndrome. The experience often blights their careers and changes their lives forever. Again, I had to wonder why.

And I had to wonder, also, why the insane governmental secrecy was still the order of the day—and why so many esteemed men of science kept stonewalling the UFO question and ridiculing reliable eyewitnesses and contactees when what these people needed most of all were sympathetic comfort and reassurance.

I don't wonder so much about any of it anymore, of course. I don't have all the answers, but I have a lot more now than I did then.

And I'm still scared.

CHAPTER SIX

Through Other Eyes

I made two other stops while I was in town. A friend works at one of the major radio stations serving the area. He showed me a "situation room" where two people were doing nothing but reviewing and plotting the reported sightings of the night before.

"It's a major flap," he told me. "We already have two hundred reports on the board and they're still coming in."

"How are you handling it for the air?" I wondered.

He looked a bit embarrassed as he replied, "We're still skulling that question."

"Meaning?"

"Well... we're sort of playing it cool right now, just tracking it and, uh, watching the reaction."

"How can there be a reaction if everyone in the media is just sitting on it?"

"That's the reaction I'm talking about. We don't want to be the only ones out there with egg on our faces."

I said, "That's gutless."

He said, "Sure it is. But we're not here for guts. We're here for revenues."

I understood that language. This was not a rock station with news headlines on the hour; it was a station whose stock-in-trade was news and commentary, and it depended on public confidence if it was going to attract advertisers. If it did not attract advertisers, it did not stay in business—and not staying in business was tantamount to cataclysm for these people. They could not afford to become a laughingstock.

It seems that there is always quite a lot to laugh at in every UFO flap because it is a phenomenon that feeds on itself. It brings out all the pranksters and gypsters and fringe lunatics who apparently cannot pass up an opportunity to climb on the bandwagon. That is the major problem for serious UFO investigations, besides which it provides all the raw meat necessary for those who prefer to ridicule serious concern.

I also looked in on the sheriff's department. If your image of a sheriff is a rawboned guy with a big hat and a star pinned to his shirt, then you do not live in Los Angeles County. This sheriff sits astride not a horse or a jeep but one of the largest and most sophisticated law-enforcement organizations in the world. His turf embraces four thousand square miles of mountains, deserts, beaches, and forests, property valued at more than 250 *billion* dollars, and eight million people living in or around nearly a hundred incorporated cities.

But I was not surprised to learn that all UFO inquiries were being handled by the public-information office.

They were cooling it, too.

I could get absolutely no information regarding the incident in Malibu Canyon, not even an admission that an on-duty officer had been involved.

But I did manage to see a guy I had met once socially who is a staff psychologist for the department. I told him that I'd talked to Grover Dalton.

He lifted both eyebrows at me and quietly asked, "When?"

I replied, "Little while ago. Are you working with him?"

He said, "Not yet."

I jotted down the name and phone number of my psychiatrist friend in Washington and handed it to him. "You should," I told him, and left him staring at my jottings.

My next stop was at the Brentwood home of Ted Bransen and Penny Laker. It was by now early afternoon. It's a sprawling ranch-style house positioned around a swimming pool and tennis court. I'd been there before. Between pool and court is a lanai that projects from a small room filled with bodybuilding equipment. Bransen is one of those who *thinks* health and physical culture but gets around to it only when it's convenient, which means probably a couple of hard workouts per month—but I guess that's better than nothing.

I couldn't get a response to the doorbell so I scaled a five-foot brick wall behind a breezeway to the garage and dropped into the backyard.

A young Oriental man dressed in domestic white was fiddling with a buried lawn sprinkler. He looked up with a start but said nothing as I nodded to him and went on.

Someone was doing laps in the pool—a female someone, it appeared, but I couldn't be sure from the angle I had.

Julie Marsini sat at a small table on the lanai, her attention riveted to some reading matter, clad only in a string bikini. Scratch everything I said earlier about "gray people" and understated beauty. In this light and attitude, the lady was worthy of full masculine attention. She did not hear my approach but also did not seem startled when I sat down across from her.

"We expected you before this, Mr. Ford," she told me with a cool look that came from somewhere in the stars, it seemed. Very, very dark eyes.

I said, "Me, too. But I had to check some details first. Is that Penny in the pool?"

"Yes."

"She seems to have recovered well."

"Recovered from what, Mr. Ford?"

"Why don't you just call me Ash."

"Recovered from what?"

"Her ordeal of the night."

"Was there an ordeal?"

She was fencing. I said, "Looked that way to me. She was staggering along a deserted road in a remote area far from home and stark naked, bombed out of her mind with something or from something. I'd call it an ordeal, yeah."

Julie stared at me through an unblinking moment, then dropped her gaze and said, "Do you have to tell her about that?"

I replied, "Doesn't she know?"

"I hope not."

"Does this happen often?"

She again raised her eyes to mine. "Does what happen often?"

"Her blackouts, memory gaps. Has it happened before?"

She was speaking so softly I was almost reading her lips as she told me, "It has become almost routine. Can you help her?"

"She needs a doctor, maybe."

Julie shook her head in a firm negative. "She wouldn't hear of it. And it is not a medical problem."

"What kind is it, then?"

"She has . . . visitations."

"From where?"

That face was a total blank. I could read absolutely nothing there as she replied, "I don't know where."

"Aliens?"

She shivered slightly but still there was no reading on the face. "Who are the aliens," she said quietly, and it was not a question.

I said, "Exactly. Who are they?"

"Maybe they are us," she murmured.

"Do they look like us?"

"Sometimes."

"What does that mean?"

"They *can* look like us. Maybe you're one." Another shiver. "Maybe *she* is one."

I was feeling a bit reckless so I asked the deadpan young lady with alien eyes, "What is the meaning of the golden triangle?"

She immediately looked away, eyes focused somewhere far off, pulled up a leg, and absently scratched a shapely ankle, said to me in a barely audible voice: "Time."

"Time?"

"Yes. It is time."

"Time for what?"

Her gaze fell to the ankle. She massaged it delicately with an artful hand, said nothing.

"Time for what, Julie?"

"Time for *them*."

"What does that mean?"

"Time to time, they come. This is their time to come."

"For what?"

She shrugged delicately, an almost imperceptible movement of glistening shoulders. "Fulfillment, I guess."

That was as far as we got with that.

Penny had come out of the pool and was walking toward us with a large white towel draped about her. I had the strongest feeling that there was nothing beneath that towel but flesh. She pulled out a chair and sat down, lit a cigarette, totally ignored my presence there, said to Julie: "The water is perfect. You must try it."

Julie replied, "You know I never swim in sunlight."

I simply was not there.

"Such a bore. Your skin will not melt, my dear. We must get a dolphin. Have you looked into that? Wait, a *pair* of dolphins. Every soul must have its mate."

"Mr. Bransen says *no* dolphins. The problems are immense. The authorities require impossible standards. They would never permit dolphins in a residential swimming pool."

"Mr. Bransen is no longer an issue. We shall enlarge the pool, remove that ridiculous cement slab for bouncing balls. Call the engineers. Meet the standards. Then we shall have the dolphins."

I tried to edge in there: "You're looking great, Penny."

Zilch.

"Mr. Bransen is very much the issue. And he grows more strident with each passing day."

I mean, I was wondering who'd *written* these lines! Talk about *stilted* dialogue!

"Cut off his funds. That will tame him."

"I'd love to screw your brains out, Penny. Yours too, Julie."

"That has been deemed inadvisable. But we must devise a rational approach to the problem."

"Ashton Ford shall solve the problem."

"Ashton Ford could *become* the problem."

"You are using my name in vain, ladies. I am in no way involved in any of this. Yet."

"This is an interesting man."

"Yes, but also a potentially dangerous man."

Penny abruptly got to her feet, dropped the towel—confirming my suspicions—and stubbed out the cigarette as she capped that conversation. "There are no dangerous men."

She went into the house, then, without a glance at me —that divine body jiggling in all its feminine freedom, leaving me with mouth agape and tumbling emotions.

Julie smiled brightly at me and said, "What did you say?"

I growled, "I said I'd like to screw your brains out."

Those great eyes fell but the smile hung in there as she replied, "That could perhaps be arranged." Then she seemed to notice for the first time the wet towel draped across the chair Penny Laker had just vacated. Her gaze darted to the pool, then around the area, in some confusion.

"She just went inside," I said quietly.

"Oh," she said.

I said it too, but silently to myself.

Either I was being conned by the slickest act in the business or...

"When would you like to attack my brains?" Julie was asking me in a playful tone.

"Entirely at your own convenience, ma'am," I replied, trying but probably failing entirely to match her mood.

"I'll let you know about that," she told me.

"When you let me know about the golden triangle," I suggested.

But she was already off her chair and moving swiftly into the house. She did not even look back or wave as she disappeared inside.

I picked up the stubbed cigarette and smelled of it, decided it was plain tobacco with no exotic ingredients added, then retreated the way I'd come in.

The little guy in the white suit was staring at me from poolside. "Great job you've got, kid," I told him amiably in passing. I was wondering if he liked dolphins as much as naked ladies.

But he gave me no clue, no clue whatever.

And I had to wonder if he was *really* Oriental. Or if he even knew what a naked lady is.

CHAPTER SEVEN

Time, Place, and Circumstance

I long ago came to the conclusion that there are no absolutes. That makes "reality" a bit easier to handle. It seems that truth is always entirely relative to the moment in which it is perceived, and "phenomena" is phenomenal only from a particular point of view—which is to say that something is true only in its own time and place, and something is phenomenal only if it is extremely unusual, extraordinary, or highly remarkable in *our* time and place.

So just how phenomenal are flying saucers?

But let's tackle "truth" first because it is easier to grab.

If I say, "It is hot today," and I am seated beside you on the burning sands of a great desert at high noon in summertime, then you recognize my statement as truth. Of course you could reply: "Not as hot as yesterday," but that is just another angle on relativity. If you are seated atop an iceberg in the Arctic Ocean and I am communicating with you telepathically from the desert, you'll have to wonder where I'm communicating from before you can decide if I am telling the truth *for me*. You already know it is not the truth for you.

Or if you have been inside a climate-controlled building for a week and I come inside with my hot-day idea, you'll either have to check with the weatherman or step outside yourself to get at the truth.

Some philosophers and even some scientists are going to want to argue with me too, when I say that truth is always relative. They will insist that *some* truths *are* absolute. Yet all their yardsticks are temporal. As much as I respect Albert Einstein and the other brilliant minds that have defined our present reality for us, none have been entirely truthful with us because none have ever possessed the entire truth, and those who know the most are the least inclined to declare absolutes.

Einstein's entire approach was to say that every event occurring within time and space is *always* relative to the *time* of the occurrence and also *always* relative to the observer. So what does that mean? It means that total scientific objectivity *in the human reality* is impossible. That may sound like an absolute in itself. If it is, then it still could be a relative absolute—relative only to the human reality in time and space.

So we can never know the absolute truth about anything. Not even about ourselves. We observe ourselves (if we do) as a continual process in space and time, an organism undergoing constant change under the stimuli of unseen and largely unimagined forces, struggling feebly to adapt and persevere in the face of continual adversity. Isn't that what life is? Does a rock struggle to exist? Does it even care whether it does or not?

Descartes, widely regarded as the father of modern philosophy, proved himself to himself by the simple statement: "I think, therefore I am." (Even more succinct in its original Latin: *"Cogito, ergo sum."*)

Even that is a relative truth. It is relative, first of all, to the definition of *I*. It is relative to the meaning of *think* and *am*. To what depths do we think? To what effect? From what cause? What *is* thought? What is it to be *am*?

Descartes died in the year A.D. 1650. What does that mean? That he is no longer thinking, therefore he no longer is? But even his "death" is relative to our perception in time and space as to what life and death are. We could now say, could we not: Descartes died, therefore we know he lived. Could we not also say: We know Descartes lived more than three hundred years ago; therefore we know that now he must be dead?

See how it all plays to the tune of *time?*

Cogito, ergo sum, from our present perspective in space and time, would no longer appear to be a valid truth for René Descartes, would it? But how can we know for sure? Maybe Descartes is still thinking, somewhere outside space and time.

Cogito, ergo sum does not even stand up to modern science. Were Descartes alive today, our brain-research people would want him to rephrase that a bit to say: "My neurons are firing, therefore . . ."

The quantum physics people would rather see *am* as a process that converts energy to matter in a standing wave of electromagnetic fields. Rocks and men are made of the same basic stuff, you see, and it all converts down (or up) to "processes in time and space" (Einstein). Both rocks and men are processes. We presume that the rock does not think but still it *is*—in our perception of *is*, anyway.

What it is, in its most obvious difference from us, is energy congealed (for awhile) in a particular packet at a vibrational density so much lower than our own that we cannot directly observe the processes occurring within that packet.

Uranium ore is, of course, a rock of sorts. And we have devised instruments that *can* observe the *is* processes within that particular rock.

The usual scenario for the natural destruction of our planet is tied to the natural processes within the sun, our star. As all stars do, ours is evolving, we are told, toward a moment in time when it will dramatically increase its burn rate for a while (during which phase its corona will engulf our planet) and then gradually subside into a cold, dense, dead body. But it will still be processing its own reality, and in time it will tick feebly away until all the chemical components have broken down into atoms and the atoms into basic particles and those presumably into whatever basic particles come from, though now with no guiding wave to give meaning (process) to their existence until another process captures them and converts them to its own design.

Our astrophysicists tell us that this sort of process will continue until all the stars have burned out and the entire universe is a drifting, cold, diffusing body. But that comes to me with just too much absolute vision. The universe did not begin with stars, I am told—not anything, anyway, that we would recognize today as a star. So the stars are just part of the process—and the process is taking you and me, pal, right along with it, and who knows from where and to where.

Descartes did not know. Einstein did not know. No man alive today knows.

So how phenomenal are flying saucers?

For the world of mankind at large, we should have reached the end of phenomenal things in the skies a very long time ago. Not that the things should not be there, but that they should no longer be regarded as phenomenal. They have been with us throughout the recorded history of the planet, and undoubtedly throughout the oral history as well.

An American Airlines DC-10 whistling across the sky above an American city in the year 1987 is not a phenomenon. It's just another routine event.

That same plane in the sky above New Mexico or Oklahoma a thousand years ago would have been a mind-blowing phenomenon signaling the coming of the gods or some such.

That is perfectly understandable and appropriate for the time frame. The inexplicable has always fueled the developing imagination of humankind—and it would appear that phenomena in our skies have forever been there to do just that. Granite carvings dated at 45,000 B.C., discovered in China's Hunan Province, depict robotlike figures and cylindrical objects in the sky. The Cro-Magnon caves in France and Spain preserve paintings from 15,000 years ago that reproduce virtually every UFO description now being recorded in our modern age, and all the ancient religious writings from Vedic and Babylonian texts to the Holy Bible describe the phenomena in the language appropriate to the time.

Virtually every civilization, every culture in the annals of humankind, have their traditions and "myths" recording the drama, from the "flying canoes" of the California Indians to the Greek Olympians and the hovering (sometimes thundering) "Lord" of Moses, throughout the world on every continent and even upon the islands at sea, each in their own way and according to their own perceptions but recognizably the same phenomena.

The modern UFO era did not begin in 1947, as commonly reported, but as early as the nineteenth century when "airships" hovered over the great population centers of the world, producing "flaps" limited only by the communications technology of the time—even earlier, being reported by Columbus, Paracelsus, and Goethe.

An entire British regiment was swallowed up by the phenomenon during World War I (and never seen again, alive or dead). I'm sure you've heard of the "Fooballs" over Europe during World War II and the phenomena associated with the Bermuda Triangle, all of which was mere prelude to the truly modern era with literally thousands of irrefutable sightings worldwide on a continuing basis for the past thirty-five years.

So it's nothing new. It has become routine. Still, each new experience is quickly dismissed by our governmental authorities and scathingly ridiculed by the academies of science. Why? Maybe someone should be asking those ladies and gentlemen why.

Aircraft are not phenomenal in our time and place.

What *is* phenomenal is the reaction of modern, intelligent men and women to the presence of aircraft in our skies.

After all is said and done, after all the comparisons of flight characteristics, wherever they come from and why they are here, the flying saucers are aircraft. They are therefore disqualified as valid phenomena.

Not that we should not be *impressed* by their presence. We should be. But the phenomenal aspects of the experience are produced by the feeling that the impressive presence of such aircraft in our skies gives us the same message it gave early man: we do not know as much as we think we know about ourselves and our world; it is more phenomenal than we think; we are not as special as we think; the world and all its systems of stars were not built for us alone.

The danger, I think, is that we then tend to see the presence in our skies with either too much reverence or too much fear. Some of us, as from time out of mind, will want to fall down and worship them. Others will want to destroy or exploit them. I cannot feel that our visitors desire either reaction, or that they deserve either reaction.

So what do they want?

That is the question I had to consider at the very outset of this case—because what *they* want may not necessarily be the same thing that *we* want. All truths, after all, are relative to their own time and place. And I was feeling very uncomfortable about *this* time.

CHAPTER EIGHT

Question of Time

I couldn't get that weird conversation with Julie Marsini out of my head. The words just kept repeating, the way the symbols had done earlier. But had she been speaking from some specific knowledge or from mere speculation? And those *eyes*. They kept looking at me, as from very far away.

Even more weird had been that exchange between the two women. Strange enough were the words, stranger yet the context of those words. They'd behaved as though I were not even present. And when Penny departed, Julie acted as though she had no memory of it whatsoever.

And what about that *dolphin* bit! Some kind of code? —a way of talking around my presence? Or did Penny Laker really want a pair of dolphins in her backyard?

I was shaken a bit, sure, but not to the extent that I was ready to leap at shadows. But what the hell did it all mean, taken in context with the events of the night? What about Grover Dalton? He seemed to me like a no-nonsense guy. I had to believe his story, not just because I could partially verify it from my own experience but because the guy would not have told such a story if he had not thought it true. I mean, a career cop is not going to invent a story like that to alibi cracking up a police car. There were too many safer lies to tell, if that was the intent.

No... the guy believed what he said.

So what was the significance of his experience?

The woman he saw in the road must have been Penny Laker. A second woman is just too much coincidence. He saw Penny. But what was she *doing* when he saw her? Fleeing? From aliens? Or had she been doing something *with* them?

Why else would the aliens "lure" him away on a futile chase through the canyon?

Evidently I'd stumbled onto Penny while the saucer was playing games with the cop. But then she'd run from *me*. Because she was disoriented and panicky and mistook me for them? Or for some other reason?

Had I really merely *stumbled* onto her—or had I somehow been directed to the scene myself?

If I could believe Julie, the experience possibly was not entirely unusual for Penny. "It has become almost routine," Julie had told me.

What had become routine?

"Visitations," said Julie. "This is their time to come."

"Weird stuff," complained Penny's husband.

"That's what happened," declared a grim-lipped young cop.

I could settle for nothing less than the sum of all that. And maybe I was allowing for a whole lot more.

* * *

I cranked up my computer and worked for several hours with the graphics that had been deposited in my head, reproducing them in silicon logic and playing with random sequences and groupings, but it got me nowhere.

The only two that had any significance for me outside the encounter that gave them to me were the triangle and a pyramid, which two are nearly the same since a pyramid is really a three-dimensional triangle. This had no particular meaning for me at the moment, though, nor did any of it stimulate any intuitive perceptions, so I ran off hard copies of the designs and arranged them on the wall behind the computer, then went for a walk along the beach.

I walked about a mile and back again, my eyes on the sky much of the time though I did not really expect to see anything unusual up there. I guess it's sort of a reflex. I had noted the same "eye on the sky" tendency in others following encounters. Only unusual thing I saw the whole time was a collection of starfish washed onto the beach opposite my house, maybe a dozen of them. I don't know just how unusual that is on California beaches, but I could not recall seeing one outside my house before.

It was about five o'clock when I returned from my walk. I should have been tired and I should have been hungry but I was neither, nor had I lost any of the mental focus which I had hoped would subside. So I went back into my study and settled onto an old leather recliner which I favor for meditation. I lay there for several minutes trying to encourage strong alpha rhythms, which is very difficult for a brain under the kind of internal stimulation I was experiencing; the alphas are strongest when the brain is awake but totally idle, weakest during focused problem solving. Actually I was trying to fake-out my left cerebral cortex and bring the right side dominant. This is sort of like self-hypnosis but with a tighter control.

The left brain of right-handed people dominates linear thinking—that is, step-at-a-time logic sequences—but it does not function well with imagery or spatial logic, the ability to see things out of sequence. However, the left brain tends to want to dominate *all* thinking and will suppress the right side to a greater or lesser extent depending on the learning experience, sometimes to the point of severe imbalance even in highly intelligent people. Since our culture has traditionally encouraged and rewarded left-brain development, we have unconsciously become a left-brained culture and sometimes it is very difficult to give equal time to the right brain, even when we consciously wish to do so. I have been working with mine for years, and I know that it is the seat of my intuitive abilities, but I still usually have to work to bring it up to a dominant position.

Anyway, that is what I was doing. And I wanted to study those computer graphics on my wall with a right-brain focus.

I had no sooner done so than I was jolted to realize that the wall arrangement was not the same way I had left it. I recognized this immediately, because I had led with the triangle and pyramidal shapes and now they were at the exact center of the display.

I saw something else significant in that brief look also, but the jolt woke up my left side and it took over the problem before I could get a right-brain fix on it. I wish it wouldn't do that. It knows that the other side is superior for this kind of work, but still it does not trust the right in matters of grave importance.

It wanted to work with *words*.

So it fired up the computer and loaded in the word-processing program and started asking questions about the symbols. We've been through the routine before, so both sides of me knew how to play the game. The left side would do all the talking. The right side would have to channel through the labyrinthine connections to the verbal centers on the left side via imagery and feelings. The result is sort of like playing a hunch or going with a flow without knowing where the flow is coming from, running with imagination, playing mental games with yourself. Even so, it can sometimes be nearly a hundred percent valid. I have learned to trust those results, but not unquestioningly.

Here's the way it went. Bear in mind that this is "keyboard talk" and that my left brain is controlling though under strong right-brain influence. The Q is a question from the left; A is hopefully a right-brain response with minimal resistance from the left.

Q—Was the graphics display really changed or are we just imagining?
A—The triangle led.
Q—Then who changed it?
A—Someone came in while we were gone. Might still be here. Better check.

I got up and looked through the house at this point. We were alone.

Q—Why was it changed?

A—To give two-dimensional sequence. These are obviously thought-forms from a being who does not reason in two dimensions.

Q—Oh great, that's wonderful. You could be my alien, couldn't you.

A—Better than you. But I don't fly saucers.

Q—Why does the pyramid follow the triangle in this two-dimensional sequence?

A—This signifies step-up. Dimensional step-up.

Q—Dimensional change?

A—Maybe. Also note the four faces of the pyramid.

Q—Are you suggesting four dimensions?

A—Or the fourth dimension.

Q—Where would that be?

A—We now have four dimensions of reality.

Q—You're figuring time, though, as the fourth. How else could we express dimensional concepts?

A—Space, time, and motion would be the basics of a matter universe. Encompassing the usual three spatial dimensions into a single expression as *space*, we then confront a three-dimensional reality where motion is the third dimension.

Q—So what is the fourth, in this concept?

A—Logically the fourth would then be will.

Q—Will what? Finish it.

A—It is finished. Will is the fourth dimension.

Q—Give it to me another way.

A—Reverse it with will as the first dimension. All else follows naturally.

Q—Let me see if—reverse the whole order?

A—Try it that way.

Q—Will, motion, time, space. How's that?

A—Not sure. Try. . . .

Q—Will produces motion. I think, therefore I am. *Am* is motion. All matter is motion. *Am* is consciously directed motion. What do I have here?

A—Transpose again.

Q—Let's see. . . . I am, therefore I think. Thought produces things. Things occupy space, define space, give meaning to space. Now. . . . What of time?

A—Motion produces time.

Q—And motion is the inevitable result of thing—no —try this: will is beingness. Thought is the expression of will. Thing is the expression of thought. Time is that which measures motion.

A—That sounds close.

Q—So will, motion, time, space. Will moves as thought and is expressed as motion to produce matter that is defined by time in the matrices of space.

A—I don't see stepped sequences as well as you do but I believe you have it.

Q—I have nothing. Take these out of stepped logic, please, and scramble them for me as a statement that is consistent with a four-dimensional reality.

A—Existence is thus defined.

Q—Try it again; less abstract, please.

A—Existence is the sum of the pyramid.

Q—Don't think I have that. Again, please.

A—The pyramid is the symbol of return.
Q—Return to what?
A—Trine plus one.
Q—What?
A—Trine plus one.
Q—I don't get that. Try it again.
A—Trine plus one. What do they want?

The right brain was worried, too. When it starts asking the questions, I know we're in trouble.

I printed out the dialogue and turned off the computer, stared again at the graphics display on the wall.

I knew more than I understood.

I was sure of that.

Which is a hell of a lot better than understanding more than you know. Small comfort. Because I did not understand a damned thing.

But I suddenly *knew* that Julie Marsini was at my front door. I knew it about one second before the door chimes sounded, and I knew it was she even before I opened the door and let her in.

I still knew a lot more than I understood.

As though to prove that to myself, I greeted Julie at the door with this surprising (to me) statement: "There is no time but that produced by things in motion."

She was looking at me oddly as she responded: "What?"

"Time is the solution."

"I see."

"Wish I did. What does it mean?"

She came inside and perched on the edge of a chair,

gazing at me through those distant eyes. "Is it like a platitude? Like, 'time heals all wounds'?"

"Not like that," I said. "More like..."

"Time is mere vibration," she said dully.

"Right," I said, "thank you."

I now understood just a tad more than I thought I did.

CHAPTER NINE

Body Language

"Sorry," I explained, "you walked in on a little conversation I was having with myself."

She looked at her feet as she replied, "Talking to yourself is okay, they say. It's when you start answering...."

I said, "Oh well, I'm certifiably crazy anyway. How far can I get beyond that?"

She looked up at me, started to say something but checked herself, stood up with a bounce, and went to the window to peer out onto the ocean. The sun was setting, streaking the sky with awesome reds and purples.

She was dressed simply in blouse and short skirt, walking shoes, carried the same tote bag that I'd noticed the first time she came calling. I could see the outlines of her thighs through the skirt as she stood at the big window, and I kept getting flashes of the way she'd looked in the string bikini.

Strikingly pretty girl, I decided, and wondered why she hadn't struck me that way the first time.

"I hope you're not crazy," she said while still gazing through the window. The mood was sober, almost somber. "Because I am really scared and I need someone really sane to talk to."

I went to the bar, said: "Then we'd better start with some lubricant. What's your brand?"

She turned to me with a tentative smile, said, "What?"

I picked up a bottle and shook it gently.

She said, "Oh. Maybe some white wine, if you have it. Or..."

"Have it," I assured her.

I floated an ice cube in a glass of bourbon, poured some Chablis, carried the drinks to the couch, invited her with my eyes to join me there. She came over and sank down at the far end—far enough that I had to stretch the arm to pass the wine to her. She sipped it delicately with no evidence that she was even tasting it and we sat there in a sort of brooding silence while she rehearsed her speech or whatever and I quietly allowed it.

Finally she said, "Maybe I'm going crazy myself."

"Maybe," I replied agreeably.

"You asked me today if..."

"Yes?"

"You were asking about Penny, and you asked if she'd been having these memory gaps and... all that."

"Yes?"

"Well she has. And I think I have, too."

"Since when?"

Those eyes hit me at full voltage then receded back to the other side of the galaxy as she replied, "Well I'm not sure. But at least for the past year. The first time it happened—I mean the first time I was *aware* it happened—

Penny told me that I had probably just left the body for a moment."

"There's a way to check that," I suggested.

"Really?"

"Yeah. Tell me exactly what you were doing the first time you noticed a discontinuity."

"Of...?"

"Of time, of experience."

"I was driving along the Hollywood Freeway."

"And what happened?"

"Well I wanted to get off on Sunset. I woke up on the Ventura Freeway in Sherman Oaks. I totally spaced twenty minutes. It was the middle of the afternoon."

"Tell me what you were thinking just before..."

"I was thinking I had to get off on Sunset. I was supposed to be meeting Penny at her agent's office."

"And where were you at that time?"

"Just a couple of exits away. I started moving to the right so I could exit and the next thing I knew I was in Sherman Oaks. I know I wasn't unconscious because it was very heavy traffic and I have a hard enough time with that when I'm fully awake."

I said, "Give me another example just like that but not while you were driving."

She immediately replied, "Well this afternoon. I was sitting in the lanai reading, and Penny was doing her pool time. I heard her in the water and I always keep a corner of the mind alerted when she is in the pool. You know, I try to stay aware of her. And I *was* aware and alert to her even though I was reading. But then it was like a snap of the fingers and you were sitting across the table from me and Penny had left the pool."

"You don't remember us sitting there talking while Penny swam?"

"No I—"

"You don't remember her getting out of the pool and joining us at the table?"

She wet her lower lip with her tongue. "No."

"She spoke to you about the dolphins."

"What dolphins?"

"The dolphins for the pool."

That struck her as funny, even through the worry. She laughed softly and said, "That would be the ragged end for Ted, I'm afraid."

"Penny told you that Ted was no longer a problem."

"Meaning what?"

I shrugged. "You don't remember any of that?"

"No. So what is happening to us?"

I said, "You began this by reminding me that I asked you today about Penny's memory gaps."

"Yes?"

"Do you remember when I asked you that?"

"Today sometime. Wasn't it?"

"Was it?"

I saw a flare deep in the eyes. She screwed up her face and gazed across the room.

I asked her, "Are you even sure I spoke about that?"

After a moment she replied, "No. I can't remember the exact..."

I said, "It was this afternoon in Brentwood. In the lanai, beside the pool. Penny was in the pool. You and I sat at the table and talked. Focus on that."

"I...I can't seem—I don't even remember you leaving."

I said, "That's because you left first. But we talked, and we talked before and after Penny left the pool. Don't you remember any of that?"

"No."

"You don't remember discussing dolphins for the pool with Penny."

She laughed again. "No."

"Or anything in particular I said while the two of you were talking about the dolphins?"

"No."

"Yet you retained what I said about Penny."

After a moment she said, "Maybe I dreamed it. I don't remember *hearing* you say it but I know you asked about Penny's memory gaps."

"As though," I suggested, "maybe someone else told you about it."

She showed me a worried frown. "Yes."

Her glass was empty. I took it from her and went to the bar to refill it. The phone rang before I could do that. The caller was Ted Bransen. He sounded far away, totally nonaggressive, frightened.

"Ford? Something crazy has happened."

"Where are you, Ted?"

"You're never going to believe this. I've been trying to reach Penny for half an hour. Do you know where she is?"

I looked at Julie. She was lost in her own thoughts, curled onto the couch, gazing across through the window at the final rays of the setting sun. I think I will always remember her just that way, in just that moment.

I told Bransen, "I don't know where she is but I'll try

to find her if it's important. What's happening? Where are you?"

"Jesus, I still can't believe it. I'm in *Buenos Aires*, Ford."

I muttered to myself, "Not another," then raised the voice to inquire, "How's the weather down there?"

"Weather's fine. I'm not. I don't know how the hell—my secretary says I called her at nine o'clock from my car while en route to the office. I told her to cancel all my appointments for the day, or so she says. How the hell did I get to Argentina?"

I sighed, looked again at Julie, said, "You don't remember."

"I do not remember a goddamn thing except driving along this strange goddamned street. I stop for directions and discover I'm in Buenos Aires, for God's sake. It's like the goddamned Twilight Zone, Ford. I've lost more than eight goddamned hours. This is crazy. I don't know *any*body in Argentina. Why would I come to Argentina?"

I asked him, "What is the last thing you remember before Argentina?"

He replied in a voice still shaking: "Goddammit, I was on my way to work."

I was mainly just trying to calm the guy. He sounded as though he could shatter at any moment. I said, "So you went on to the airport instead and hopped a flight to anywhere. Happens all the time, in this high-pressured world we live in. Just relax and—"

"I don't have my fucking passport!" He was screaming at me. "I didn't take any fucking airplanes! Don't you understand what I'm telling you? I'm on my way to the office. Okay? I'm driving along and suddenly realize I'm lost, don't recognize anything. I stop and ask and they say fucking *Buenos Aires,* for God's sake. I'm not crazy. I'm telling you I'm not crazy!"

I said, "Try to cool it, Ted. Of course you're not crazy. It is not crazy to have a spot of amnesia. It is not—no airplanes? Are you saying . . . ?"

"My car, right, same car, the Bentley—I'm driving to work in the Bentley and next I know it's eight hours later, I'm still driving the Bentley, but now I'm in Buenos Aires. Amnesia doesn't move a car from Santa Monica Boulevard to Buenos Aires in eight hours, does it?"

I said, "Ted, listen . . ."

"I'm in all kind of trouble, dammit. No passport, no sticker for the car, can't explain how I got into the country. I can't tell these people I was just driving to work, can I? What the hell do I tell them? They'll put me in a straitjacket if I . . ."

I said, "Hold the phone, don't go away. I'm going to give you the number of a man to contact there locally. Now call the guy. He'll understand and he will not put you in a straitjacket. Just a minute, I have to get the number."

I put down the phone and went into the study, found the name and number in Buenos Aires I was looking for, picked up the phone in there, and passed it on to the bewildered Ted Bransen. He said, "Thanks," in a barely audible voice then asked me, "What is going on here, Ford?"

I replied, "Not sure. Just call that number, tell the guy the truth, he'll help you."

"Is this a doctor?"

"Not a medical doctor, no. But he is a scientist and he will understand and he will help. So call him."

"Okay. Try to find Penny. Tell her I'm okay, but dammit, don't tell her about this."

I hung up before replying, "She could probably tell you about this, Ted." I stared at the telephone for a moment just trying to size the thing in my mind, then I went back to the other room and hung up that phone.

Julie was now standing at the window.

And standing right outside the window—well, actually, hovering at about twenty yards off the deck, was a bright blue oval light about twelve feet in diameter. Another stood slightly above and several hundred yards to the rear, and it was much larger. It is very difficult to describe these things because the colors are unlike any color we usually experience on earth and the movements are unlike anything we usually see moving through our skies. Even the light itself has a different quality, otherworldly, totally alien.

The small saucer was doing a little dance.

Just sort of like a graceful wobble, tilting on its axis in a rhythmic dance.

And Julie's body was sort of like duplicating that motion.

The implications were fairly obvious.

They were conversing.

CHAPTER TEN

Wish Upon a Star

At this point, things become a bit jumbled in my mind, amost dreamlike, but I knew and I know that I was not dreaming. It was happening in the real world and in real time. I just did not know how to define "it."

I think I saw the small saucer moving closer to the house but there was no sound. It just sort of floated in to hover with the leading edge almost touching the deck outside. I turned to check out Julie at that moment, who was just standing there now like in a trance and softly humming a tune like a lullaby but none I could identify.

When I looked back toward the saucer again, a ramp had come down from the center of it and these little creatures were scampering across it. They had very quick movements with occasional freezes, like squirrels do, or like someone who is not well coordinated, or maybe like mechanical devices. Maybe they were robots. Whatever, they had the ability to run, walk, fly, and hover with a minimum of effort, and they moved very quickly.

I have a very difficult time describing these entities, so please bear with me—and I don't even know what to call them, so let's stick with entities. I'd say around four feet tall, sort of thick bodies but very skinny limbs. I think there were four limbs but I wouldn't swear to that. No obvious waist or neck; I don't remember hands or feet. The eyes were what you really noticed. About the size and shape of small eggs, very black and glittery, took up most of the face. Not sure if what I saw at the sides of the heads were ears or antennae. No nose, very strange mouth—just a slit from ear to ear. They are almost comic-looking and so were their movements. No sounds that I recall. I think more than likely they were robots.

I don't remember them coming inside. I do remember feeling very alarmed. Okay, scared; I was just about frozen with it. I do remember thinking that I should not resist but just let it happen and hope for the best. They were fully in charge of the situation and I knew it. No physical resistance was possible, I was thinking, so I may as well relax and go with it.

That is what I tried to do.

I don't know how many there were. But they were all around me. They lifted me up, I guess, and carried me out—and I probably weigh more than the whole bunch put together. Come to think of it, I'm not sure that they lifted or carried me. I don't think I walked but also I don't remember being touched. It was more a floating sensation. I don't remember being taken out of the house or entering the saucer. I do remember a cramped room in very bright light but no sensation of movement. I believe the small saucer than rendezvoused with the larger craft because I also remember "floating" along this very long ramp, like going up into the bowels of a very large structure.

I went through a couple of air locks—or something like air locks—and then I was on my feet, I was alone, and I was walking along this brightly lighted corridor toward a huge, domed room. A Michael Rennie type of character *(The Day the Earth Stood Still)* walked out to greet me. He wore a jumpsuit and soft black boots. The suit was made of some soft, thin fabric that fit him like skin from his neck to his ankles and wrists, no cuffs, a sort of glowing metallic silvery color.

He was about my same height and build and he wore a very gentle and reassuring smile. The lips were a bit thin but I have seen lips that thin on earth; the eyes a bit almond-shaped and I could not discern an iris, but not all that noticeable; ears rather small and shaped sort of like upside-down from ours.

We talked just like people.

He said, "Hello, Ashton. Thank you for coming without a fuss. Please be assured that we mean you no harm. You may call me Donovan."

I said, "Is that your real name?"

He replied, with a chuckle, "No, but it's close enough. You would have trouble with our pronunciation."

He led me into the domed room and over to a large oval window. I could see the lights of Southern California, from Santa Barbara to San Diego, spread like sparkling jewels far below.

"Do you recognize that?" he asked me.

I said, "I've never seen it from this height but I know where it is."

Donovan smiled and said, "Stay right here," then he

went to a control panel about twenty feet away and did something there.

I felt a slight lurch, barely noticeable. Donovan called to me from the panel, "Now what do you see?"

It sure wasn't Southern California below me now. For one thing, the image was reversed. As though we had swung around the earlier scene to regard it from the other side.

I looked at him and shook my head. He did something else at the panel and I experienced another faint sense of movement. When I looked out the window again, the scene below was much closer. I could pick out moving streams of lights that had to be cars moving along highways—a number of bridges, tall buildings.

I said, in a voice much too quiet for him to have heard, "L.A. to New York at the snap of a finger."

But he heard that. He called over to me, "Very good," and then as I was watching we blipped over to London for a closeup on Big Ben, to Paris and the Eiffel Tower, to Honolulu and Diamond Head.

When Donovan rejoined me at the window, California was again directly below.

"How do you do that?" I asked him. "You just broke every physical law in the universe."

He laughed quietly and replied, "Not quite. But we keep trying."

The guy was very "human." Wouldn't take much Hollywood makeup for him to be indistinguishable in any crowd on earth. I felt like a mental pygmy in his presence, though. He must have read my thoughts because he told me in very gentle tones: "We are not that different,

Ashton. Not as close as brothers, perhaps, but certainly closer than cousins. Your origins are my origins."

I asked, "Where would that be?"

He said, "It no longer exists and has not during the time of man on earth, so how could I tell you in terms that you would understand."

I suggested, "But you know all about man on earth."

He smiled. "More than you might believe. Oh, you are a troublesome bunch. But we love you nonetheless."

I said, "Well that's comforting. A lot of people think you mean to eat us or something."

He smiled again and replied, "Please be assured that we are confirmed vegetarians."

Before I could think of anything else to say, we were joined by another couple.

Both female.

One was Julie, dressed just as I had last seen her.

The other was Penny Laker, or a pretty close double. She wore an outfit identical to Donovan's and on her it was a knockout.

Julie's eyes looked a bit glassy, otherwise she seemed okay in every respect. She gave me a tight smile and said, "Isn't this exciting?"

I replied, "Better than Disneyland."

The four of us laughed.

Penny touched my hand and said, "We have important work, Ashton. Will you help us?"

"Time to conquer earth?" I asked, trying to smile as I said it.

She did not quite know how to handle my humor, passing it to Donovan with a little frown.

He told me, "We could manage it ourselves, but it is

best we don't. Best for all concerned. We cannot and would not force you. Ashton, why should we conquer you? We already..."

I said, "Already what?"

He smiled, squeezed my arm affectionately, told me, "We already love you. Be assured that we mean no harm to any resident of earth. Will you work with us?"

Well there was only one thing I could say in sanity; right? So I told him, "Guess I'm already part of it. May as well go for broke. What do you want me to do? Please don't ask me to publish a UFO newsletter."

Donovan laughed.

Penny frowned.

Julie clutched my arm and whispered, "Be careful."

Next thing I remember, Julie and I were walking hand in hand down the long ramp. I was feeling great, almost elated. Julie seemed to be upset, though; she was trembling and maybe sobbing a little.

That particular part is like a mere snapshot in my mind.

The next I know, Julie and I are embracing on the floor of my living room and she is moving her fully clothed body against mine in considerable urgency. There are tears on her cheeks but she is smiling through them as she says to me, "I find it convenient now, Ashton, that you attack my brains."

And that, pal, was only the very front of the night.

CHAPTER ELEVEN

Brain Drain

I have since been able to reframe my memory and to thus realize that there were various real-time validations buried in the experience. For example, it was about eight o'clock when I was taken aboard the saucer. I calculate that from the fact that the sun was setting when Julie arrived at my house and night had fallen shortly thereafter.

If the whole thing had been purely a mental experience, I doubt that my delusion would have been well enough organized to take the earth's time zones into account. Yet when Donovan whisked me off to London, which is eight time zones east of Los Angeles, Big Ben was showing the time as 4:12 and it was dark there so it must have been A.M.

Then when we backtracked from Europe to Hawaii in a twinkle of time, the relative position of the sun was appropriately rolled back to a couple of hours before sunset.

Of course—even allowing the experience as real-world

and real-time—those apparent leaps through space could have been electronically staged illusions. I have had to consider the possibility that the "oval window" was actually a large view screen and that Donovan was playing tricks with my head. He had seemed a bit evasive when I asked how he did that.

My feeling throughout the encounter, however—that is, the feeling that came through the memory of it—was that Donovan had been trying to convince me of the reality of the experience and to give me some hint of their technical capabilities. I don't know why he would think that important—or why they would even bring me aboard—if the only intent was to deceive me. What possible purpose could they have for something like that? If, on the other hand, they were genuinely trying to recruit me for some sort of service, then the actions were logical.

I had to go for logic, so I had to go with the idea that I had been recruited.

Recruited for what?

I could not remember being asked to do anything specifically or agreeing to do anything.

But then, also, there were identifiable gaps in my memory.

So...they had planted something in my mind?—something that would operate like a posthypnotic suggestion?

What the hell could they have programmed me to do for them?

That was a worry. He'd said that they would not force me—and why would he have gone to the trouble to ask for my cooperation if the intent all along was to strongarm my subconscious? But it was still a worry.

During some earlier UFO investigations I had talked with several very convincing individuals who'd claimed to have been abducted by aliens and taken aboard their craft. I had felt that I had to suspend judgment in each of those cases because: a) the stories were so damned bizarre and yet; b) the individuals had so obviously undergone terribly traumatic experiences.

In trying to compare my own experience with those, I could recognize various parallels. Yet I did not feel particularly traumatized. Other than the fact that I was seized and transported without my permission, I had not been abused or mistreated in any way. Even so far as being "seized," hadn't I long welcomed such an experience in my mind?—and if they had a way of knowing what was in my mind, couldn't that connote "permission" for what would seem a kidnapping from our point of view but perhaps only a form of invitation from theirs?

And of course I "came back" in a most delightful way, wrapped up with Julie in a sensual wrestling match on my living room floor. Could that have been programmed too? If so, the program had been written for two because we were both half crazy with desire and it took a long time to get fully sane—a *long* time—and we displaced most of the furniture in that room during the process. It was as though we were developing our own version of the Kama Sutra while also testing the human anatomical design for innovative concepts in sex. I am still wondering where we got all the energy and stamina because it seems that we compressed an entire lifetime of sexual experience into about three real-time hours.

I do know that we were both hoarse and too exhausted to move when the thing had run its course. The room was a wreck, and so were we both. I *crawled* in search of a cigarette and righted several overturned lamps along the route, pulled myself upright at the bar, and grabbed cigarettes and a bottle of Seagram's, then crawled back and knelt beside my sobbing counterpart.

I lit a cigarette and luxuriated in the exhalation even though it further overburdened my respiratory processes, then asked, "Why... the hell... are you... crying?"

It took her a while to work the words through as she replied, "Because... so... happy... dammit."

I giggled like a schoolboy and took a belt at the bottle, swished the whiskey around inside my mouth before swallowing it, got my breathing under control, then reminded her, "You said... it was... convenient time."

Julie feebly rolled onto her stomach and rested her head on crossed arms, said to me: "Play it... again, Sam."

I laughed and replied, "Fat chance, kid. This tune... is all played out."

She groaned, "Ditto. Kidding." She moved onto her side and rearranged her head to peer up at me. "What time is it?"

I squinted at the wall clock, told her, "Nearly midnight."

She groaned, got an elbow under her and elevated to a sitting posture, curled in her legs, said, "It was still daylight when I got here. What was in that wine?"

I replied, "Hey, kid, if what we just had came out of the wine, I want a patent on that sumbitch."

She giggled weakly and took a drag from my cigarette, coughed, told me, "Guess you did promise me a brain drain, didn't you."

"Purely as a figure of speech," I replied. "I think we brought it back from the saucer."

"Where?" She was giving me a sort of dizzied look.

"From the flying saucer or whatever, mother ship, whatever."

Her eyes widened. "I didn't dream it?"

I replied, "When did you have time for dreaming?"

She said, "I meant...during our—while we were—I think I'm still confused. Could I be dreaming now?"

I said, "God I hope not."

"Well I mean...all that really happened?"

"What do you remember?"

"I just...remember...this weird place. Wait! No! First, I *saw* it right outside! Then...this strange place and...and Penny was there. Wearing a uniform. We talked. I don't remember what about. Was there another man? Or was that you?—in a uniform. Oh. Oh. I feel very scrambled inside."

Scrambled, yeah.

That was the word.

I was scrambled a bit too, but maybe I had a better handle on it all only because I was more accustomed to unscrambling things in my head.

I helped the confused and physically exhausted woman to her feet and walked her to the bathroom, adjusted the shower, left her to her privacy, and returned to the living room for another taste of bourbon.

I was not even aware of my own nakedness as I went to the window and stood there with the bottle in my hand to gaze into the heavens.

The night was clear and starlit.

Far up and far out, at about a forty-five-degree angle

above the horizon, a particularly bright star commanded my attention. I stared at it for several minutes, during which time I would have sworn that it changed positions very slightly several times.

Could have been an airliner out of LAX streaking for Hawaii. If so, it sure hung a long time in the vision, and it did not seem to diminish in size or brilliance.

Toward the end of that brief vigil, I imagined that the thing winked at me. Twice. Off, on; off, on again.

I raised the bottle and waved it over my head.

It winked again, slowly. Off, wait a beat; on, on a beat; off and gone.

It was an airliner.

Sure it was.

CHAPTER TWELVE

Scenario X

Once you get past the UFO question—is it or isn't it an intelligently controlled vehicle of some sort?—you can settle down to the practical questions. Where are they from? How do they get here? What do they want?

It is not even a totally safe bet to declare them extraterrestrial. They could be based right here on earth—beneath the seas, in very remote areas, even within great hollows of the earth. I've heard all those theories soberly considered by educated persons.

I always preferred to believe that they are not based on the earth. They could have bases in other parts of the solar system. It seems that our moon would make an excellent platform in space. Various planets and/or their moons could also provide a stable physical environment for the establishment of spaceports. They could even have their own artificial satellite implanted independently in our solar system.

All of those solutions beg the ultimate question, of course: what is their *origin*?

Donovan told me, "Your origins are my origins."

Swell. So how does that help the understanding?

Either they cloned us and left us here millennia ago to shift for ourselves, or they are an echo of a much older civilization on earth than any of us have yet discovered. Maybe Atlantis really happened, or something similar. Maybe these guys were off adventuring in other neighborhoods of the galaxy when hell came to earth, wiped away every vestige of culture and technology, and left only a few pitiful survivors brainwashed by centuries of terror and unimaginable hardship to begin again the human effort to dominate the earth. So maybe Atlantis or something like Atlantis was the real Eden. And maybe these guys have finally returned home only to find a totally alien planet, and they're trying to figure it out or to decide how best to merge back in with us.

Don't like that?

Well maybe we have a much more distant common origin. Donovan said the place ceased to exist before man began on earth. Maybe our star was dying and everyone had to bail out of that solar system. Maybe they had hundreds, even thousands, of years warning so had plenty of time for an all-out technological effort to launch some lifeboats into space. Maybe the lifeboats got separated—as lifeboats often do—and they ended up in different worlds. Maybe the one that came to earth crash-landed, or maybe everybody was sick, or maybe it was forty generations after the launch before the setdown on earth and all the occupants had lost their marbles or regressed or whatever scenario you prefer to explain the almost total loss of knowledge and technology.

Note that I said *almost* total loss.

There are evidences around the globe of extremely ancient civilizations that seemed to know more than those who descended from them. Take even the "creation myth" of Genesis which scholars now believe to predate the Babylonians and even the Sumerians, who lived in roughly the same place but at different times, the Sumerians being older. Their language is the oldest written language on earth, and the origins of the peoples themselves is lost in prehistory. Their written language was in cuneiform script and today's scholars cannot forge a relationship between that language and any other known on earth. Wonder where it came from, and where it went.

The creation story told in the older writings in Genesis (there are several such stories, sort of overlapped and bastardized by a succession of later writers) shows what would seem to be an amazing understanding of cosmology from such a primitive viewpoint. So much so that there really is no basic conflict between the general story of creation in the Bible and the generally accepted scientific theories of today, until you get to Adam and Eve in the garden at Eden (which was a much later embellishment on the story).

Of course the language is quaint from our point of view because the story had come through the mists of time and can be interpreted only through our present understanding of language, but the true scholar is left with the eerie feeling that he is reading a partially bastardized *memory* of greater truths once known.

Beginning with a universe of chaos and darkness from

which the earth was cast, then developing by successive stages the appearance of order, then of plants, then animals, and finally man—the reader encountering this fragment of a sentence would not know if it were quoting a scientific account or Genesis. It happens to be both. And it represents the very earliest recorded thoughts of man regarding his origins.

So where did prehistoric man get all this understanding?

Maybe it was one of the few tattered fragments left in a shattered lifeboat, and maybe the survivors were too busy with the elemental tasks of adapting to an alien and terrifying environment to devote much time to anything else, especially to cultural luxuries. What did it serve you to know how the world was made or how a shattered craft was powered from another world if wild beasts are stalking you and you are cold and hungry? If you have no tools and none of the materials with which you are familiar, what good is technology?

Does the average man or woman alive today have any really valid idea of how images are flashed through space to come alive on their television screens? Can anyone reading these words *build* a television station or even a receiving set with bare hands and raw materials? Can anyone working alone and without modern facilities build even a transistor? So if you are shipwrecked like Robinson Crusoe will you devote your time to trying to figure out how to build a television receiver or will you forage for food to stay alive?

If that is how it all began with man on earth, then suffice it to say that he foraged for food and forgot about the fineries. We are here today as evidence of that, if that

TIME TO TIME / 77

it is. And now our long-lost brothers-in-kind have found us. Evidently their ancestors fared better than ours, because they still have the technology of survival in space that ours lost. They would approach us with great care and discretion, not with bands blaring and arms outstretched to these primitive throwbacks who cannot even find peace among themselves.

To continue the scenario, put yourself there for just a moment and try to relate it to something in your own experience. You live in Omaha and you discover as an adult that you have a long-lost sibling who was stolen from his cradle by Gypsies. You learn that he is alive and living as a terrorist in the Middle East; he is a religious fanatic committed as a holy mission to the destruction of the Great Satan, Uncle Sam. Already he has bombed school buses and killed hundreds of innocent people. What are you going to do—and how are you going to approach this wild man, if at all?

We could go on with many such scenarios, one for every theorist who has ever thought about the problem.

I really do not know what good the scenarios do.

We are being visited.

Our visitors are vastly superior to us in many ways.

They probably have the capability of destroying us one and all overnight.

Even our governments around the world are afraid to admit that they are here or that they even exist.

Our scientists too, by and large, scathingly ridicule any suggestion that they do not know all that there is to know about everything in the universe. Since they know nothing whatever of the technology that brings these visitors to our world, obviously these visitors exist only in the minds of self-deluded persons.

I shall speak later of two prominent spokespersons for the scientific establishment who best exemplify that turn of mind, and I will give you samples of their reactions so that you may see for yourself the depths to which the human mind can travel in trying to shape its own reality. For now, just trust me that it is true, subject to later verification.

Our educators are in the same boat as the scientists; by and large they are essentially one and the same and their behavior is the same for the same reason.

Ditto for the churchmen, for different reasons but with the same result.

So to whom do we turn to get the truth?

There's the rub, my friend.

There are none to turn to.

You've got to figure it out for yourself, and your very survival may depend on how well you do that.

CHAPTER THIRTEEN

National Anathema

Donovan had said to me: "Why should we conquer you?" And he started to say more, as though to answer his own question: "We already..."

"Already what?" I'd asked.

"Already love you," he replied.

Doesn't really fit, does it. I call that a recovery from a near blunder. He almost told me more than he wanted me to know.

So. Already what?

Already *conquered* us?

Already *own* us?

Already what?

I was quietly pondering the question when Julie emerged from the bathroom wrapped in a towel. The sight of that immediately tossed my mind back to that encounter beside the pool with Penny Laker, and I was mentally rehashing that weird experience when Julie playfully slapped my bare bottom and pushed me toward

79

the shower. She seemed totally collected, refreshed, in charge of herself again.

I doubted that a mere shower could have that effect on me, but I definitely needed the shower. I spent about twenty minutes under the stinging spray, by which time I was at least beginning to think rationally, and I emerged to find a Spanish omelet and scalding coffee awaiting me at the dining table.

Evidently she was as hungry as I, and we consumed the food with a minimum of conversation. Each time our eyes met she smiled and dropped her gaze as though embarrassed by the encounter. And she kept checking and adjusting her towel. I finally removed mine and tossed it across the room; said, "Who needs it?"

She released hers at the underarm cinch and rearranged it across the lap without looking at me. Beautiful body, yeah. Glowing flesh, sculpted breasts, very inviting.

I said, "That looks much more comfortable."

Eyes down, she murmured, "It is. Thank you."

We concluded the meal in silence. I lit a cigarette, offered her one, she declined. She still was avoiding my eyes. I said, "What's bothering you?"

"Nothing is bothering me," she replied.

"Queen Victoria," I suggested gently.

She smiled and shook her head. "No, I've never felt confined by that standard. Guess I—well maybe so. Maybe I'm wondering what you think of me."

"Does it matter?"

"That's bothering me, too. It does matter."

I chewed it for a moment, then asked, "So what do you think of me?"

She raised luminous eyes to mine, smiled, said: "You

touched depths in me that had never been touched before. I think it confuses me. I'm wondering if it confuses you."

I said, "I think you're talking about falling in love."

"Maybe. I feel sweet sixteen again."

I said, "Couldn't have been so long that you would have forgotten how that feels."

She said, "Oh yes it could."

Those eyes were looking at me from far across the galaxy. I found myself shivering inside and knew that I had to ask *the* question.

"Are you one of them, Julie?"

"Yes. But then so are you."

"In what way?"

"In every way. They've awakened you now, as they awakened me."

"Why?"

"Why? Because it is time again."

"Time for what?"

"I don't know. I just understand that it is time again."

"Time for something very important."

"Yes."

"We're supposed to help."

"I think so, yes."

"How?"

Those luminous eyes fell to an examination of the tablecloth. Suddenly I was into her. I can't explain how this happens because I do not understand it myself even though I have had such experiences throughout my life. I just knew suddenly that our minds were touching and that I was knowing what she was knowing. Not in words but in images, feelings, emotions.

I encountered a great sadness in that interchange, an

almost overpowering sense of regret, coupled with images of great destruction and widespread tragedy.

It came and went in a flash, but I had the images in my mind now, and I had the great sorrow.

Julie said, very quietly, "You just invaded me, didn't you."

I replied, now totally enveloped in her mood, "Not intentionally. Sorry. Can we talk about it?"

"No."

"Then would you like to make love again?"

"Yes."

I stood up and took her hand and led her to my bed, and we did it again—the right way, this time—with tenderness, with feeling, and with respect.

And, afterward, Julie said to me in a whispery voice, "Life is not a game. It is a terribly complex mission, and this is our only reward."

"*This* is?"

"Love is."

I understood then why she wanted so desperately to be in love. Why we all do. And why some of us opt out for unsatisfactory substitutes easier to achieve. Find a negative human expression and you have encountered one of those substitutes. That was my illumination, there between the sheets with a fellow alien from the far side of the galaxy. But I still did not know what *time* it was.

More than thirty-five years ago, at the very dawn of the modern UFO age, a scholarly Russian Jew from Israel landed on our shores with a manuscript that would forever challenge man's view of himself, of his own history, and of his solar system. The man's name is Immanuel

Velikovsky, and his *Worlds in Collision* was destined to ignite a fire storm of controversy that now stands as the most shameful attempt to suppress nonpolitical ideas since the Inquisition.

Velikovsky's great sin was that he chose to accept as literal truth the vast treasury of written history which modern scholars universally regard as religious myth. Another great sin was his vast intellect and fearless determination to state his views into the teeth of academic dogma and arrogance; his intrusion into the jealously guarded temples of science.

Even so, the hysterical reaction by some of the most eminent educators and scientists must have gone far beyond anything this quiet scholar could have anticipated. The language used to denounce him—even before his ideas had been published—was ferocious to an extreme unmatched in modern times, harkening back to the dark days when scientists themselves were being anathematized by the church, and to the same spirit that burned Giordano Bruno at the stake and inspired Galileo to recant in order to escape a like fate.

Velikovsky did not write about or even mention flying saucers; indeed, he had undoubtedly never heard of such phenomena when he arrived in New York shortly after the end of World War II. But his story is relevant here as a stage setting for the later fire storm over UFOs, and I believe you will find it interesting as an insight into the functioning of some academic/scientific minds.

He was a medical doctor and psychiatrist with a fascination with biblical lore and an inherent sensitivity to the broad historical overview of man and his environment. Whether his reconstruction of history was right or wrong was never the issue. It was the *implications* of that reconstruction that caused the panic in so many institutional minds and made his very name a sore point to academicians (to this very day) who have never read a line of his book.

Velikovsky was not an astronomer or physicist, but the mere publication of his ideas was obviously highly threatening to the entire academy of astronomers and physicists here and abroad.

He was not an historian, or a sociologist, or a naturalist, or an anthropologist, archaelogist or geologist, yet many of these almost with a single voice arose to denounce and castigate *the man* without even coming close to a direct contact with his writings.

What caused such hysteria in our academic and scientific communities?

Velikovsky took the biblical events and other "myths" as a true account of real experiences of real men and women sharing together the real history of this planet. He then looked for logical explanations within the natural world to verify this real history. His brilliant investigation took him into the heavens as well as into the earth, and his conclusions were spectacular.

For example, though not an astronomer and with no credentials whatever to make such a statement, Velikovsky theorized that Venus did not begin its planetary existence as the other planets did, that in fact Venus did not occupy its present orbit around the sun until very recently, that in fact it was torn from the body of Jupiter by a violent upheaval within that planet and was loosed into the solar system as a comet that made several close passes at Mars as well as Earth, and settled into its present orbit during the recorded history of mankind. That "recorded history" is contained within the legends and myths for all to see.

The whole astronomical world "knew" and had long accepted the thesis that Venus has a surface temperature below sixty degrees Centigrade and that frigid Jupiter is buried beneath miles of ice. With all that learned conviction, it is easy to see how the institutions would laugh up their sleeves at the novel conclusions by Velikovsky that both planets must be quite hot, but it is not easy to understand the anger and hostility with which these conclusions were met.

Velikovsky's ideas were, of course, anathema to the body of professionals who enjoy the prestige and respect normally accorded our men of great learning. If Velikovsky was right then these guys were dummies and undeserving of their robes and honors—or so they seemed to feel.

The most prestigious American astronomer of the time, Harlow Shapley of Harvard (who apparently led the attack on Velikovsky) stated in a letter dated May 27, 1946: "If in historical times there have been these changes in the structure of the solar system, in spite of the fact that our celestial mechanics has been for scores of years able to specify without question the positions and motions of the members of the planetary system for many millennia fore and aft, then the laws of Newton are false. The laws of mechanics which have worked to keep airplanes afloat, to operate the tides, to handle the myriads of problems of everyday life, are fallacious. But they have been tested completely and thoroughly. In other words, if Dr. Velikovsky is right, the rest of us are crazy."

Shapley said it; I didn't. But Velikovsky was right. The pity is that none of these pillars of science would even *consider* the evidence. All of their protests were based on mere hearsay of Velikovsky's theories, long before the book was actually published.

And, for the shameful aspect, the storm of protest was geared to a single goal: the suppression of the ideas. Shapley led a broad institutional attack upon the proposed publisher of the Velikovsky manuscript, Macmillan Company, which was highly vulnerable to academic displeasure because of its large investment in textbook publishing. In a letter dated January 25, 1950, to the publisher at Macmillan, he tried to get the message across in a sly way: "It will be interesting a year from now to hear from you as to whether or not the reputation of the Macmillan Company is damaged by the publication of *Worlds in Collision*. Naturally you can see that I am interested in your experiment. And frankly, unless you can assure me that you have done things like this frequently in the past without damage, the publication must cut me off from the Macmillan Company."

Another member of Shapley's club, Dean McLaughlin, Professor of Astronomy at the University of Michigan, wrote Macmillan on May 20, 1950: "The claim of universal efficacy or universal knowledge is the unmistakable mark of the quack. No man can today be an expert even in the whole of geology or the whole of astronomy. There is specialization within specialties. I do not mean that we are ignorant of all fields but our own; I do mean that we are not equipped to do highly technical original research in more than several distinct specialties for each scientist. But no man today can hope to correct the mistakes in any more than a small subfield of science. And yet Velikovsky claims to be able to dispute the basic principles of several sciences! These are indeed delusions of grandeur!"

The entire point of McLaughlin's letter was in protest to Macmillan's "promulgation of such *lies*—yes, *lies*, as are contained in wholesale lots in *Worlds in Collision*."

Strange, isn't it, that the professor states in the same letter: "No, I have not read the book."

This is just a tiny sample of the unprecedented conspiracy to suppress a publication and which succeeded to the extent that Macmillan passed their hot potato off to Doubleday, which has no textbook division. But the club even went after Doubleday.

In a letter to a Doubleday subsidiary dated June 30, 1950, Fred Whipple—Shapley's successor at the Harvard Observatory—worded a sharply sarcastic broadside at the new publisher in discussing a public account of the matter: "*Newsweek* has unwittingly done the Doubleday Company a considerable amount of harm. They have made public the high success of the spontaneous boycott of the Macmillan Company by scientifically minded people."

Whipple then went on (in the same letter) to suggest a similar treatment of Doubleday: "There will be no revision of *Earth, Moon, and Planets* (a book by Whipple) forthcoming so long as Doubleday owns Blakiston (the subsidiary), controls its policies, and publishes *Worlds in Collision*."

Yet in a statement printed by the *Harvard Crimson* on September 25, 1950, Harlow Shapley said: "The claim that Dr. Velikovsky's book is being suppressed is nothing but a publicity promotion stunt. Several attempts have been made to link such a move to stop the book's publication to some organization or to the Harvard Observatory. This idea is absolutely false."

What were these great men so frightened of?

Velikovsky's thesis was to the effect that global cataclysms had fundamentally and repeatedly altered the face of the planet Earth during historical times, that the terrestrial axis had shifted, magnetic poles reversed, even a different orbit established.

In horrific convulsions, the oceans had replaced continents, Earth's crust had folded, massive volcanoes spawned new mountain chains, lava flows of up to a mile thick covered vast areas of the planet, climatological changes converted lush gardens to frozen tundra, and forests became deserts.

Civilizations collapsed in a wink and whole species disappeared as gigantic tidal waves swept along the continents, crushing and burying everything in their paths.

Stunned human survivors recorded the events as best they could, and those records survive today for any who will look and see.

Velikovsky looked, and he saw and reported it again. He also theorized a logical explanation, based entirely on the evidence, of how it all came about. Jupiter gave birth to Venus, which became a comet and roamed the solar system for eons before inevitable celestial mechanics brought the huge mass into a collision orbit with Earth.

It is not even important to my point here that Dr. Velikovsky's radical theories have been largely vindicated (though not on purpose) by new discoveries during our space age. Venus is a hot body with a very thin crust, as

Velikovsky concluded, and it does rotate in a retrograde motion, again as he concluded. Jupiter is a very hot body —now even possibly thought to be a dim companion star to our sun—and it is a radio source, as Velikovsky theorized.

Many other of Velikovsky's theories, regarding electromagnetism and sunspots and various other phenomena of our solar system, have been vindicated.

None of that is the point.

The point is that the entire scientific/academic community rose up to crush these ideas even before they could be promulgated, and with the aim of suppressing them rather than meeting them head-on in true scientific curiosity.

This is one example of a human phenomenon, the curious workings of the mind having to do with intellectual arrogance and survivalist instincts.

We will meet another example later, in the discussion of a similar conspiracy to suppress through ridicule all reasonable debates and/or researches of the UFO question.

Then we'll try to figure out why these people are so frightened.

Or do we already know why?

CHAPTER FOURTEEN

Star So Bright

Julie and I had fallen asleep in each other's arms. I was awakened at a few minutes past two by a bright light flashing through the bedroom, like automobile headlights can do if you live close beside a roadway.

I woke up with a start, thinking, *Oh hell, they're back*.

But I couldn't hear anything unusual and Julie was sleeping peacefully, so I also wondered if I had merely awakened from a dream. I carefully disentangled myself from Julie so as to not disturb her sleep, sat up and lit a cigarette, and knew that I was going to have a hell of a time getting back to sleep again, even as tired as I was.

I'd had only a couple of drags off the cigarette when I heard a movement somewhere in the house. I was preparing to investigate that when a figure appeared in the bedroom doorway. It was no more than an indistinct silhouette in the darkness but I knew that someone or something was there.

So I hit the bed lamp.

Julie awoke with a jerk.

Penny Laker was standing in our doorway. I thought at first that she was still in "uniform" but as my eyes adjusted to the sudden light I could see that she was wearing a skintight workout suit similar to the one I'd seen before. It occurred to me in that same moment that the tights were also very similar to the uniforms, and I again wondered if the whole saucer thing was mere delusion. If so, then we had an even larger phenomenon, involving the workings of the human mind, to consider in trying to understand a universal delusion shared by every culture upon the globe.

All that went through the mind in a flash and even as Penny spoke: "Julie? Is the party about over? Can you take me home now?"

That voice was quavery, frightened, confused, and finally embarrassed. Very convincing. The real Penny Laker was back, or at least the one I'd known in the past.

I said, "We'll be right out, Penny."

She retreated from the doorway but I could still hear her frightened breathing as I pulled on my pants and growled at Julie, "Make it quick, huh."

Julie nodded her head in understanding and I left her to pull herself together while I went to talk her boss back into the terrestrial world.

I hit every light switch we passed to dispel all the darkness inside there as I took Penny to the kitchen. I sat her down and small-talked without letup while building coffee and until Julie came to my rescue.

All the while the actress kept darting glances everywhere and obviously trying to pull the corners of her mind together in some understanding of where she was and why.

I would not have considered asking where she'd been and how she'd gained entry to that locked house. She seemed to be under the confused impression that she'd been asleep on the couch.

Julie came in fully dressed and apparently ready to travel, the tote bag slung from her shoulder. We had coffee and talked idly for several minutes but Penny was still obviously very confused when they departed.

Julie hung back at the doorway to brush my lips with hers and whisper, "I'll call you."

I whispered back, "Do that. And keep a close eye on your boss."

Hell, I just couldn't figure it. Oh in medical terms, sure, it could figure. Dissociation, split personality, etc. If she'd gone to a shrink and told him about the memory gaps and waking up in strange places and stranger situations without remembering anything about flying saucers or aliens, sure—there would be no problem diagnosing the disease.

The problem—and I'd been aware of it for years—is that in dealing with any disease of the mind, the therapist is always using one imprecise term to define another. With all the talk about chemical imbalances, inherited tendencies, complexes, and the whole wide range of mental disturbances, nobody really knows where the crazies come from or what initially produces them. There is not even now a broad consensus among medical people as to how best treat the symptoms, and apparently there is no such thing as a true "cure."

The unhappy truth is that no one really knows what

they are dealing with. They talk about treating the mind without knowing even what or where the mind is. They are really treating the brain, or trying to, and that organ is of such unutterable complexity that any tinkering with it is as likely to hurt as to help.

Which is why I get so upset with people who experiment on themselves with mind-altering drugs. It scrambles the associations so delicately balanced to produce a vehicle for consciousness in this space-time framework. Screwing with the brain with chemicals is equivalent to going at a computer with hammer and chisel, and I shudder at some of the things done under the label of medical science.

I could only guess at the confusions within Penny Laker's brain, never mind what was causing them.

Because I really did not know who Penny Laker was.

Hell, I did not know for sure who *I* was.

The human experience is a fragile thing. Presumably everything that we now know, that we have ever known, and that we shall ever know in this lifetime, is the result of the electrochemical exchanges within our gray matter. Nobody really knows why the neurons fire, or how, or to what ultimate effect. We fire, therefore we think. We fire, therefore we see, and hear, and taste, and smell, and feel. We perceive our entire reality completely within the head; that is where we meet the world, and dissect it item by item, then reconstruct it as an *image* in the mind. That *image* is knowingness, yet all we ever know is the image.

We "know" by comparing images, by relating new ones to old ones held captive in something we choose to call *memory,* and yet even the process of searching memory and comparing images is electrochemical and made possible by the firing neurons.

A neuron, you know, is fantastically complex.

It is much more mysterious than a flying saucer or interdimensional space. It is literally a mind within a mind, and there are many *billions* of them in each human brain. Yet many are specialists, designed to fire only under specific circumstances and for specific effects, and the final *image* we get from millions of simultaneous firings is totally dependent upon which ones fire and in which sequence.

Don't ever take yourself for granted.

You are more marvelous and more intricate than you could ever imagine. And you are *not* the images that appear to you. You are that which produces the images, the whole intricate, marvelous, unimaginable complex of neuronal *processes* that reproduce the universe within your skull.

But surely you are more than that, too. It is my considered opinion that you are that which produces the processes, but I cannot begin to imagine the ultimate implications of that idea.

So ... what is it all about?

What do *they* want?

I am not even sure who "they" are.

But I believe that the human brain is a multidimensional space-time model of the universe. That being the case, we at least have the potential for being as *smart* as *they*. And it seems entirely likely, yes, that our origins are the same.

My mind was thus occupied when the telephone rang and Ted Bransen again presented himself to my consideration. The women had been gone for only a few minutes. He yelled, "Have you seen Penny?"

"She and Julie were just here," I replied.

"What time is it there?"

"Little after two," I told him.

"Shit, I must be halfway around the world. It's past seven o'clock here! Listen, I'm worried about Penny. I'm retaining you to protect her. I mean hire all the people you need but I want her covered twenty-four hours a day."

I said, "Ted, that's not necessary. She—"

"Don't tell me what's necessary," he yelled. "I thought she was just going fruitcake but now I don't know, I mean there's more to this than meets the eye. But I guess you know all about that, don't you. This guy you sent me to. He's a UFO expert. You knew that, huh."

"That's why it's not necessary, Ted. There's no way to protect against this sort of thing. But if it will make you feel any better, I am on the case and I am trying to figure out what is going on and why. I suggest that you just try to relax and—"

"What the hell kind of talk is that? How can I relax? This friend of yours is taking care of the paperwork for me. I don't know what his contacts are but he's already in touch with the right people. They're going to put me on a plane at ten o'clock. I should be back in there before midnight, your time. I don't know, I think I might have to go to New York first and get a flight out of there. Listen, this is crazy stuff. It's going to take me half a day to get back home. And I'm just gonna sell the goddamn Bentley. No way am I going to pay—where do those people get off with crap like this! Your friend says I'm not the first. What is this?—practical jokes from outer space? I still can't believe it!"

I said, "Well, they did get your attention, didn't they."

"I still don't know what to believe. But I am worried about Penny. I think this is some of what she's been going through. So you sit on her tight until I get back there."

I said, "Sure, sure," and hung up.

Hell, I couldn't even sit on myself.

It seemed the edge of idiocy to try to play bodyguard against alien power when even the combined might of all our armed services plus all our police agencies appeared to be so helpless in the face of it that they wouldn't even admit the problem. But since I was probably up for the night, anyway, I figured I may as well spend the rest of it parked outside the Laker mansion.

If there were goings and comings there, I wanted to know about it even if I did not know what to do about it.

So I showered and shaved and made tracks as quick as I could. It was exactly three o'clock when I took the Maserati out of the garage and set off for Brentwood.

I knew exactly where it was.

All I had to do was follow the star that was hovering high above it.

Someone else, it seemed, was already sitting tight on Penny Laker.

CHAPTER FIFTEEN

A Little Cloud That Tried

It is very hard for the thinking mind to settle around something like this. Even coming into it with the mind totally open, even with considerable investigation and research behind you, when the human mind is confronted with genuine phenomena the very strong tendency is most usually to try to explain it in conventional terms. It is no wonder that the scientist becomes so closed-minded and protective of the status quo; the whole movement of mind seems directed toward preserving its own baselines and allowing the addition of new information in carefully stepped increments and with great discrimination. This is indeed the scientific method, so one bolsters the other in the effort to keep reality within closely defined bounds.

What we mean by the term "mind-blowing" is that some radical new perception is threatening the base structure of the reality-model that we carry around inside our heads. We apparently need that base structure in order for the mind to function per its design, to compare the present with the past, and make intelligent decisions based on that comparison.

When something comes along to "blow away" that base structure, then with what do we compare that event in order to decide its meaning intelligently? Right; no comparison is possible, so the natural tendency is to scale down the event to a comparative level.

That is what the normal mind does, and there are many brilliant automatic techniques built in to help us do that.

So you find yourself wondering if you *really* saw or heard or felt or otherwise experienced what you thought you did. You question the *validity* of the experience because that is how you keep in touch with your model of reality. And you can become highly creative in constructing rationalizing arguments that reduce apparent phenomena to a level comfortable for the mind.

So although I was probably ninety-eight percent absorbed into this experience, a very stubborn two percent of intellect was still trying to argue that it was not really happening. Something *else* was happening and I just was not seeing it in its true light. Soon, I would. Soon, I would tumble to some new explanation to make the whole thing entirely mundane and manageable.

Manageable, aha. There's the key to that whole two-percent attitude. We humans like to have at least the illusion that we are in control and running things. We are a species that has come to life with the apparent ability to manipulate our environment and bring the world to us on our own terms. We feel strongest and safest when we are doing that, weak and defenseless when we cannot. That's the whole story of relationships between mankind, is it not? Who is in charge here?

If the flying saucers are for real, then obviously someone else or something else might be in charge. Many of us are not willing to relinquish that kind of power even to God.

This was my thinking as I sat my lonely vigil in the Maserati outside the Laker estate, and I give it to you here to show that I was trying to handle the problem with a thinking mind, that I was not totally subjective about the experience.

Because a lot of crazy things began happening almost immediately thereafter.

The usual morning fog was moving onshore, and Brentwood is not that far from the Pacific. Actually Brentwood is one of the posh Los Angeles neighborhoods sitting west of Beverly Hills and north of Santa Monica, sort of nestled into the foothills behind Pacific Palisades (Ronald Reagan's ex-home). There appeared to be about a fifty-foot ceiling over this particular area, with occasional drifting patches right down on the deck. I had to work the wipers occasionally to keep the windshield clear.

I had been there for nearly half an hour, parked about a hundred feet off the property, when I noticed a peculiar shift in the layer directly above the Laker house. An irregular-shaped piece broke out of the base of the clouds and gently settled toward the house. It came to rest no more than ten feet above the roof, sort of flattened out on the bottom and top, and quietly spread itself over the entire house. It looked like fog to me but I had never seen anything like that kind of formation with any fog I'd ever seen. Living at Malibu, I see a lot.

After a minute or so, the bottom edge began unraveling

into long streamers that totally engulfed the house in a matter of seconds. I sat stupidly watching, and wondering what kind of environmental forces would make a pocket of fog act like that. I kept expecting it to dissipate but it did not dissipate, so after another minute or two I ventured from the car and went down for a closer look.

I have been into some pretty heavy paranormal stuff, which you already know if you've been following my cases, but I have to tell you that this event ranked very high on my eerieness meter. I could not even see the house now, although other houses nearby were clearly visible, as well as closely bordering trees and shrubs. The outer lawn in front was visible, but it and the sidewalk and the driveway extended for only about ten feet before absolutely disappearing behind the fog bank. I know that for a fact because I stepped straight along that sidewalk expecting the visibility to rise with me as I went along into it, but it did not. I stepped through a *curtain* of fog and straight into another world. And now I desperately needed my two-percent objectivity.

A very interesting story from World War I, which I briefly mentioned earlier, deserves to be told in detail at this point because it is a close parallel to my own experience that night in Brentwood so may help the credibility factor here just a bit.

The event was reported by numerous professional observers but dismissed on the spot and all eyewitness accounts buried in secret document files until recently when a group of surviving observers demanded on the fiftieth anniversary (during the UFO age) that it be publicly reported.

TIME TO TIME / 101

The incident is referred to as "the vanishing regiment" and it occurred in August 1915, during the Dardanelles Campaign near the Turkish seaport of Gallipoli. The regiment that vanished was the British First Fourth Norfolk, which had been dispatched to reinforce the troops at Hill 60. The phenomenon was witnessed by twenty-two men of an ANZAC force, three of whom signed the following affidavit on the occasion of their Fiftieth Jubilee:

> The day broke clear without a cloud in sight, as any beautiful Mediterranean day could be expected to be. The exception, however, was a number of perhaps six or eight "loaf of bread" shaped clouds —all shaped exactly alike—which were hovering over "Hill 60." It was noticed that, in spite of a four or five mile an hour breeze from the south, these clouds did not alter their position in any shape or form, nor did they drift away under the influence of the breeze. They were hovering at an elevation of about 60 degrees as seen from our observation point 500 feet up. Also stationary and resting on the ground right underneath this group of clouds was a similar cloud in shape, measuring about 800 feet in length, 200 feet in height, and 200 feet in width. This cloud was absolutely dense, almost solid looking in structure and positioned about 14 to 18 chains from the fighting in British held territory."

We are talking, here, a "cloud" nearly the length of three football fields, forty feet wider than one, and as tall as a twenty-story building. A "chain" is a field-surveying term of linear measurement; eighty chains are equal to a mile, so the cloud was positioned about one fifth of a mile *inside* the British lines. The ANZAC observers were watching as the men of the First Fourth Norfolk began their march up Hill 60 to join the fighting. But the First Fourth never got there. Ever see one of those old war movies with a proud and feisty British force marching snappily into the fray? Picture that here, please; it helps the graphics.

> When they arrived at this cloud, they marched straight into it, with no hesitation, but no one ever came out to deploy and fight at "Hill 60." About an hour later, after the last of the file had disappeared into it, this cloud very unobtrusively lifted off the ground and, like any fog or cloud would, rose slowly until it joined the other similar clouds which were mentioned in the beginning of this account. On viewing them again, they all looked alike "as peas in a pod." All this time, the group of clouds had been hovering in the same place, but as soon as the singular "ground" cloud had risen to their level, they all moved away, northwards, i.e. towards Thrace. In a matter of about three-quarters of an hour they had all disappeared from view.

This, of course, from trained observers who by the year 1915 certainly knew the difference between a cloud and other things that may appear in the sky. And note how slowly the "clouds" stole away. The affidavit concludes:

> The Regiment mentioned is posted as "missing" or "wiped out" [inside their own lines?] and on Turkey surrendering in 1918, the first thing Britain

demanded of Turkey was the return of this regiment. Turkey replied that she had neither captured this Regiment, nor made contact with it, and did not know that it existed. A British Regiment in 1914–18 consisted of any number between 800 and 4000 men. Those who observed this incident vouch for the fact that Turkey never captured that Regiment, nor made contact with it.

Not only some eight hundred to four thousand men vanished but this was a self-contained combat unit fully equipped and prepared to fight. I leave it to your own imagination what the First Fourth encountered within that cloud, how a fully equipped army would have reacted to a bizarre situation, *why* they vanished, and to what conceivable fate.

I give it to you here because it makes my own incident in Brentwood paltry in comparison. I myself have found comfort in that comparison. But not much.

CHAPTER SIXTEEN

Dancing in the Dark

I still sometimes find myself wondering why I stepped so unhesitatingly into that "fog." It would seem that the natural mechanisms for personal survival would have intervened somehow, dictated caution and at least a tentative advance. In reconstructing the moment in my mind, I find no memory of fear or even disquiet although I had gone to investigate something *because* of its unusual character. But I stepped right into it without a qualm.

Maybe those men of the First Fourth later asked the same question of themselves. And I guess I will wonder all my life what they found inside *their* cloud.

I found a different world.

I experienced a temperature differential at mid-stride, one foot in predawn, misty, chilly coastal California and the other in a bright, pleasantly warm Wonderland. The scene was both pastoral and aquatic, with green-banked canals crisscrossing the entire field of vision as far as the eye could see.

The sky was not blue but faintly purple. Reddish-tinged, puffy clouds appeared and disappeared in rapid sequence as though the entire sky were being projected as a study in time-lapse photography, yet there was nothing unreal about it. There was no sun in that sky—but a panoply of luminously twinkling stars, with an intensity equal to Venus at her brightest, seemed to be the light source, with an effect somewhere between twilight and high noon on a cloudless day in spring, bright but soft and no shadows upon the landscape.

There were trees unlike any I had ever seen anywhere but still vaguely familiar here and there, like viewing abstract art; the same with riotously colored fields of flowers, great bowers of flowering shrubs, towering vines climbing into the purple sky like seabeds of kelp rising from ocean depths.

I was startled by the scene but, again, not alarmed. I walked right into it. I do remember halting and looking back after maybe a dozen strides, expecting to see the fog bank behind me. Instead, I was centered in the scene and there was nothing behind me but more of the same.

I remember thinking, there's no way back, but even that came with no sense of alarm.

There was no pathway or roadway, nothing whatever to suggest a desired direction of travel, no artificial structures to indicate human presence or activity. It seemed at first to be an entirely static scene, with myself the only sentient creature within it.

I was aware of a greatly heightened sensitivity within myself, as though all my senses were extended and tingling into the contact with this strange environment. I was breathing easily and walking effortlessly; I felt light, almost buoyant; the air was sweet with odors and it seemed that I could even *feel* it touching my face. I felt great, almost exhilarated, and I was thoroughly enjoying my walk though I had no idea where I was or where I was going.

I came onto a canal and strolled along its bank for a while before noticing that the water was totally transparent yet I could not see anything representing a bottom in its depths. The other bank was forty feet or so distant and though the canal wound through the landscape, it seemed to hold that same width for as far as I could follow it with my eyes. I could see things moving deep beneath the surface but they were so far away I could not identify definite shapes or patterns to the movements.

I stopped and sat down close to the water's edge and lit a cigarette. It tasted terrible. I tried to poke the cigarette into the water to put it out, but it would not penetrate the surface. It was like trying to shove a finger into stiff Jell-O.

I was thinking how very weird that was, yet I accepted it without even reaching for an explanation. It was simply water that could not be penetrated from its surface.

But then I very quickly received a demonstration that the water was not solid like Jell-O. I saw a form approaching leisurely from the depths; it grew larger and larger on a direct approach to where I sat until finally I recognized the object as a dolphin—well, sort of a dolphin.

It broke the surface no more than three feet from where I sat, only its head projecting from the water although I could see clearly the entire body as though it were suspended in air before me. This dolphin had very human-like eyes and its face was highly expressive.

I did not see its mouth move but I distinctly heard with my ears a very pleasant voice speaking in my language, incredibly gentle and melodious.

"I *thought* I saw something up there. Hello. What are you called?"

Now I know this must sound to you like Alice in Wonderland or some such, but it only made me wonder again where Lewis Carroll got his idea for that story in the first place. I mean I had a divided consciousness here. I knew that it was a bizarre experience, but at the same moment I was going along with it as though it was perfectly natural and commonplace. I mean, you know, talking to a dolphin.

I replied, "I am called Ashton Ford. Who are you?"

"Ashton Ford," the dolphin repeated. "That is a pleasing sound. I am called Ambudala." This is a phonetic approximation. It was a definite four-syllable sound but with musical components that do not translate into writing.

I said, "Pleased to meet you. I seem to be a little lost. I thought Penny Laker lived here but I can't seem to find her house. Do you know Penny?"

Ambudala replied, "Perhaps I have heard the name but I would not know her if she is a house-dweller. If you would rest a moment, however, I will consult the Knowledge and seek a solution. Will you wait?"

I said, "Sure. Thanks. I'll be right here."

Ambudala slipped back beneath the surface. The water simply closed on him. There were no waves or ripples, no disturbance whatever at the surface to mark his point of departure. But I saw him streaking into the depths until he was too far away to see with the unaided eye, and a moment later I saw him returning at a slightly different angle. He moved with incredible swiftness. If he'd been in a tank at Marineland, moving at that speed, he could have jumped hundreds of feet through the air when he reached the top. But he came to a smooth halt, again with only his head exposed.

He was a bit breathless, though, as he reported to me, "Yes, Penny Laker is a house-dweller but not in this domain. You have obviously broken the harmonic. The Knowledge respectfully requests information as to how you accomplished that."

I countered with a curiosity of my own. "Can you distinguish that I am a different species of life than you?"

He immediately replied, "Oh, more than that, Ashton Ford. Yes, yes, much more than that. Can you not distinguish that you are an entirely different *reality* than I am?"

I said, "I'm getting that impression, yes. Do you see many like me come through here?"

"Time to time, yes," the dolphin replied. "Will you provide the requested information?"

The thing still seemed entirely real to me.

I told Ambudala, "Sorry, I don't know a thing about it. You'll have to ask Donovan."

"Oh, oh, oh," the dolphin replied, highly impressed and seemingly in some kind of rapture over the very sound of that name. "You are sent by Donovan?"

I said, "Well..." and was trying to think of some way to respond to that question when Ambudala again returned to the depths. This time he was a mere streak through a crystal medium. And he did not return.

But that was okay. Because moments later I caught another motion, this one in the purple sky, a flashing like lightning inside a cloud except there was no cloud in that region of the sky, and the motion became an approach as a small disclike object hurtled in from the horizon. It came to a smooth halt at about a thousand feet directly overhead then began a wobbling descent and landed beside me.

It was rounded on the bottom and flat on top, like a cantaloupe cut in half, made of shiny metal with a bright sheen like chrome. No more than three feet across, with a shallow cockpitlike scoop in the very center—again, like the cantaloupe after you've cut it and scooped out the seeds. The cockpit was padded and lined with a soft material, almost like automobile upholstery. There were no instruments, and there was nobody I could see controlling the thing.

But Donovan's voice came from it and told me, "Get aboard, Ashton."

I stepped aboard and sat down. A clear dome came up from the periphery of the cockpit and closed an inch above my head. There was no sound and not even much sensation of motion as the disc lifted off and tilted into an incredible climb.

I had a perfect view of everything around me, above me and even below me, and it seemed that I was putting the purplish atmosphere behind me.

I was streaking through space, in total darkness now in

less time than I can relate it, among the stars, one of the stars myself as far as I knew.

I could hear sounds like tinkling glass, and they even began to take on a form and substance like orchestrated music.

I had the impression of dancing—dancing through outer space, a velvety nowhere—yet at the same moment aware that I was moving faster than anything ever thought possible within my mind—and I believe that I blacked out for a moment because I remember experiencing extreme physical stress, like you would get from great G-force, and I felt much more comfortable when I came out of the blackout though now the sense of speed was such that I wondered if I had broken the light barrier.

It was not undirected motion. I knew that I was streaking along a precise path and toward a precise goal but that was the limit of my "knowing."

And obviously not nearly as much time had transpired in the tiny saucer as I'd thought, because toward the end of that I suddenly realized that I was holding a lighted cigarette, and I knew that it was the same cigarette I'd tried to extinguish in the impenetrable waters of the canal in Ambudala's domain because I recognized the way it was bent from the attempt.

I tried to sample the taste of the cigarette but could not advance it toward my mouth. I was locked absolutely motionless within that hurtling sphere, could not move even a finger.

It came to me, then, that I was not breathing.

How could I not be breathing yet still be alive?

I was *thinking*, dammit, and thought occurs within

time, doesn't it?—so how come I could get away with thinking and not breathing at the same time?

I experienced a sensation of slowing, then of standing still, then a gentle settling as a leaf falls from a tree. I was still in absolute darkness, and now in absolute silence.

I said aloud, "Where am I? What's going on?"

Donovan's voice came from somewhere inside my own skull: "You got lucky, pal. This is where you get out."

The dome opened.

I climbed out from utter darkness, feeling tentatively for a toehold with one foot still in the cockpit, and stepped down into swirling mists. I was in Penny's backyard, the wall of the carport directly behind me. I lifted the cigarette to my lips and took a deep drag and it tasted mighty sweet.

So where the hell had I been?

I had no memory of walking into that fog with a lighted cigarette. The only one I remembered lighting was the one beside the canal just before Ambudala had appeared.

Where the *hell* had I been?

"Obviously you broke the harmonic," Ambudala had told me, as though it were not all that unprecedented an event.

I could not have imagined all that in the space of thirty or so paces from the curb to Penny's carport.

Could I?

Maybe so.

But I had good reason to think about it a while before coming to a decision.

That reason was in Penny Laker's swimming pool. It

was much larger than I'd last seen it, and there was no more tennis court.

And a pair of unusual-looking dolphins were having a nice swim within its crystal waters.

Where the hell *had* I been?

CHAPTER SEVENTEEN

Friends and Lovers

They looked like regular dolphins to me. But I knew there was no way that the pool could have been enlarged by any conventional method since the last time I'd seen it, not unless Penny had help from a Navy Seabee battalion or some such. Even so, it would have taken that much time to add the water alone, never mind all the construction work. Actually it was an entirely new pool. The one I'd seen the day before was a standard cement pool, no more than twenty by fifty feet, with an ordinary cement patio surrounding it. This one was well over a hundred feet long, made of Plexiglas or some other synthetic material with built-in artificial boulders, surrounded by luxurious lawn, and it looked very deep throughout. Underwater lighting provided a uniform glow from end to end.

Just for the hell of it, I tried submersing the cigarette in it, then sheepishly looked for somewhere to dispose of the soggy butt.

114 / Don Pendleton

The dolphins came over to check me out. I checked them out, too; neither looked like Ambudala but I figured I'd give it a try just for the hell of it. I smiled at both and said, "Ambudala?"

Both whistled in reply and took a turn around the pool in opposite directions then came back for another look.

"What are you called?" I asked them. "Jambalaya? Crawfish Pie?"

They grinned at me and went away.

I was thinking that I would have grinned too, in their place. Must have thought I was some kind of nut. Dolphins are highly intelligent, you know. Perhaps, it is said, more intelligent than man in many ways. I always get the feeling, around dolphins, that they are merely indulging our superiority complex. They know that we want them to be intelligent toys so that's the role they play, though all the while wondering how we could be so stupid as to believe that we are the smarter species.

I went over and sat in the darkness of the lanai, lit another cigarette, tried to pull my head together about the events of the past little while. According to my watch, I had just about had time to walk from my car to the lanai via the carport with a brief stopover beside the pool. About three minutes had elapsed.

But that could not be possible.

I could not have *dreamed* that much in three minutes.

So could it be possible to hallucinate such a vivid and elaborate experience in a single flash? I doubted it. And what about the pool? Could it have been built and filled and stocked with dolphins in less than a day?

I had a terribly sinking feeling at that point of my inquiry. I looked again at my watch. It's just a plain old-fashioned sweep-hand Timex without a calendar. So how could I automatically assume that only three minutes had elapsed since I left my vehicle? Maybe it had been twelve hours and three minutes, or twenty-four hours and three minutes; hell, it could have been *days* since . . .

If that spanking new pool could be a reliable measure of time, it could have been *weeks*.

"Lost time" is a common feature of UFO close-encounter experiences. And look at Ted Bransen, who'd been whisked from a Los Angeles street to Buenos Aires, car and all, in what appeared to him as a flash of the eye but turned out to be a matter of hours.

So where had Bransen *been* during those missing hours? Forget Buenos Aires. Where had the guy been during the transit? I had assumed that they'd loaded him car and all into a big saucer and carted him down there. But maybe that was too mundane an explanation. Maybe those big saucers moved interdimensionally; maybe they didn't need to use our space at all except for minor corrections for spot locations. Maybe they did not even need the saucers for their hocus-pocus.

I had not been in a big saucer. Had I? Hell no. I stepped through the fog and straight into another world.

But wait a minute!

It only *looked* like fog. How the hell could I know what I stepped into? Maybe I stepped into total oblivion, momentarily, and I simply had no memory from the one step to the next. Maybe it all *had* been a dream—even a very long dream—and that was the only memory available to bridge the time gap.

So where had I been?

I think I was really hoping for a time gap as an explanation of the experience, but there was no time gap. I discovered that very quickly. The lights in the lanai came on, I heard the patio door open, and Julie Marsini stepped out with a revolver in her hand. She was pointing the gun at me so I sat very still until she identified me.

"Oh God!" she cried. "I'm glad it's you! I don't know what I would've done if I'd found a strange man in the lanai."

I muttered, "Nice to see you, too. What day is this?"

"What?"

"Did you and Penny leave my house just a short while ago? Or was it a few days ago?"

She carefully deposited the revolver on the table, sat down across from me, and fiddled with her robe as she peered closely at me and said, "Don't tell me. Now it's happening to you."

I said, very quietly, "Not just me. Have you seen your new pool?"

She said, "What?"

"Pool." I jerked a thumb over the shoulder. "Check it out."

She checked it out from where she sat. Formerly the lanai had marked the transition from pool-patio to tennis court. Now it was all pool. She gasped and rose out of her chair, dropped back into it abruptly, said not a damn thing.

I was waiting for her verbal reaction, so I said nothing, too. We sat there quite a while saying nothing. Finally I asked, "Where's Penny?"

"Asleep," Julie whispered, still gazing toward the new pool.

"Sure about that?"

She looked at me then as she replied, "I just looked in on her. Why?"

I said, "Because someone delivered her dolphins."

"What?"

I said, gently, "Get it together, kid. You know what I said and you know what I'm talking about."

"There are dolphins in the pool?"

I nodded. "There are."

She said, "Ashton, this is crazy. I was out here just a little while ago. None of this was here."

"Has Penny been out here?"

"No. She slept all the way home, in the car. I had a hard time getting her out of the car and into bed. Why?"

"Did she tell you how she got into my house? Where she'd been? Anything at all?"

"No. I told you, she slept all the way home. Why?"

I growled, "Hell, I don't know why. Don't expect brilliant questions from me in the face of all this. I just know that I was here yesterday and heard you and Penny talking about getting dolphins for the swimming pool. You told her it couldn't be done because the pool didn't meet the standards, or something silly like that. So now there's a new pool and a pair of dolphins in her backyard. I guess I am still trying to find something sane in all this. I desperately need to find that."

Julie had been all but dumbstruck from the moment she became aware of the new pool. But now she laughed and lightly said, "I'm sure there's a perfectly logical explanation. You know Penny, when she sets her mind to something."

I said, "Uh-uh. Not in our reality, Julie, there is no logical explanation for that pool. Even supposing some whirlwind contractor came out and somehow did this job overnight, there would be some evidence of all that work. There is no such evidence. And hell, it would take days to fill that hole with water, even using fire hoses. No. Here is one we cannot explain away."

"Are there really dolphins in it?"

I took her hand and led her to the edge of the pool. Jambalaya and Crawfish Pie came racing immediately to the spot and did a spectacular leap for us.

I said, "There you go."

Julie said, very quietly, "We're in big trouble. This is against the law, I know."

I said, "That's the least worry. Did you see the fog?"

"Sure I saw the fog. Drove all the way from Malibu in it. Why?"

I said, "Not that fog. I mean the one that settled over this house a short while ago. The one that brought the dolphins."

Julie took a step backward, gave me a rather detached stare, and replied, "Why are you doing this?"

I viciously shook my head, hoping that would clear it, and asked her, "Exactly what am I doing?"

"All these questions, this third degree. You know perfectly well why the dolphins are here."

I said, "Then I guess I forgot. Why don't you refresh my mind."

"Just thinking it doesn't make it so."

I said, "Julie, what the hell are you talking about?"

"Thinking it's not doesn't make it not."

I said, "Hey..."

"Just accept what you have to accept and let it go at that!"

"Julie . . ."

She was walking slowly back toward the house, tossing these little aphorisms at me over her shoulder. But I'd already seen the explanation in her eyes, that glassy stare which I had noted there before. God only knew what this girl had been through already to test her sanity. I was just a new kid on the block, still wet behind the ears—what could I know of sanity tests? So maybe this was her way of handling it. They were not aphorisms; they were more like pressure valves, vents for the mind—or maybe simple affirmations that all is well despite ample evidence to the contrary.

Whatever, she was walking out on me.

"I'll call you sometime, Ashton. Thank you for a lovely evening. I'll tell Penny that you looked in on us."

I said, "Julie, for God's sake, cut it out. Let me help."

"Oh you've been most helpful. Thank you so much. It's okay now. Thank you. I'll call you."

That's the standard kiss-off in this town. Nobody ever calls when they say "I'll call you." It means "Don't call me." It means "Farewell and fuck off."

I said good-bye to Jambalaya and Crawfish Pie and went out through the carport.

Just for the hell of it, I touched the hood of the Maserati to verify that it was still warm. It was.

I got in and hit the starter but the engine would not crank. I was cussing under my breath with the decision that I would have to raise the hood and check the battery cables but something else stopped me before I could get a foot on the ground.

The "something else" happened inside my skull, between my ears but not through my ears: "It is all right, Ashton Ford. The vehicle shall function now. Try again."

That "voice" sounded familiar, yeah, but I couldn't be sure. I turned the key in the ignition again and she kicked over immediately with a smooth purr.

I muttered aloud, "Thanks, Ambudala."

"You are quite welcome, but it is not Ambudala. Nor is it Jambalaya. We are called Sinjasan and Marbotisun. Your reality is now our reality. May we be friends?"

I replied aloud, "Sure, sure. Welcome to my reality, kids. But I think you were probably much better off with your own."

So much for affirmations and mind-vents.

I cut the ignition, locked the car, and went back across the street. It was time, I figured, to talk turkey to a couple of dolphins. Or maybe just to talk old times.

CHAPTER EIGHTEEN

Poor Fish

I can relate this story to you only in terms of the subjective experience that unfolded in my own consciousness, along with whatever objective commentary I may use to dimension or explain or rationalize that experience to myself. You should bear in mind, as I have tried to, that a respectable school of professional thought regards all UFO phenomena in purely psychological terms. Of course it is often impossible to reconcile certain manifestations of the phenomena with the psychological theories, such as the actual physical movement of objects and people from one location to another, physical imprints upon terrain, and actual physical effects (radiation poisoning, etc.) suffered by contactees.

Such physical effects apparently do not deter those who insist upon the psychological syndrome, who invariably find a way acceptable to themselves to dismiss such evidence from their studies. I regard that as an interesting psychological study in itself, since it shows how far even a highly educated and intelligent professional can travel to accommodate his own bias while studying the "delusions" of others.

Let me give you an example of what I mean by that. The "Midwest flap" occurred during early August 1965. An area of some several hundred square miles was subjected to strange "nocturnal lights" which appeared on three successive nights. Police officers and various other reliable witnesses across several states reported the phenomena. The Air Force's Project Blue Book, the only official UFO investigatory body, received direct reports from other Air Force commands as the thing was going down. Those reports were logged by the Blue Book duty officer, a Lieutenant Anspaugh, who made the comprehensive report reproduced in part below.

> 1:30 A.M.—Captain Snelling, of the U.S. Air Force command post near Cheyenne, Wyoming, called to say that 15 to 20 phone calls had been received at the local radio station about a large circular object emitting several colors but no sound, sighted over the city. Two officers and one airman controller at the base reported that after being sighted directly over base operations, the object had begun to move rapidly to the northeast.
>
> 2:20 A.M.—Colonel Johnson, base commander of Francis E. Warren Air Force Base, near Cheyenne, Wyoming, called Dayton to say that the commanding officer of the Sioux Army Depot saw five objects at 1:45 A.M. and reported an alleged configuration of two UFOs previously reported over E Site. At 1:49 A.M. members of E Flight reportedly

saw what appeared to be the same formation reported at 1:48 A.M. by G flight. Two security teams were dispatched from E flight to investigate.

2:50 A.M.—Nine more UFOs were sighted, and at 3:35 A.M. Colonel Williams, commanding officer of the Sioux Army Depot, at Sydney, Nebraska, reported five UFOs going east.

4:00 A.M.—Colonel Johnson made another phone call to Dayton to say that at 4:00 A.M. Q flight reported nine UFOs in sight: four to the northwest, three to the northeast, and two over Cheyenne.

4:40 A.M.—Captain Howell, Air Force Command Post, called Dayton and Defense Intelligence Agency to report that a Strategic Air Command Team at Site H-2 at 3:00 A.M. reported a white oval UFO directly overhead. Later, Strategic Air Command Post passed the following: Francis E. Warren Air Force Base reports (Site B-4 3:17 A.M.) a UFO 90 miles east of Cheyenne at a high rate of speed and descending—oval and white with white lines on its sides and a flashing red light in its center moving east; reported to have landed 10 miles east of the site.

3:20 A.M.—Seven UFOs reported east of the site.

3:25 A.M.—E Site reported six UFOs stacked vertically.

3:27 A.M.—G-1 reported one ascending and at the same time E-2 reported two additional UFOs had joined the seven for a total of nine.

3:28 A.M.—G-1 reported a UFO descending further, going east.

> 3:32 A.M.—The same site has a UFO climbing and leveling off.
>
> 3:40 A.M.—G Site reported one UFO at 70° azimuth and one at 120°. Three now came from the east, stacked vertically, passed through the other two, with all five heading west.

I go to all this trouble merely to show you how far others are willing to travel in order to deny the evidence before them. And I quoted official Air Force sources—men in high positions of responsibility who are entrusted with the defense of the nation—to show you that no one is immune to the treatment.

The entire Midwest flap of 1965 was totally dismissed by the official explainers as "stars seen through inversion layers." How far can we push credibility to suggest that scores of highly trained professionals whose business it is to distinguish between optical illusions and threats to the security of the nation went into a near panic produced by optical illusions?—and, if it is true, how secure can any of us feel that our national security is in good hands?

I don't really worry that much about the latter consideration because a Cal Tech astronomer laughed when I asked him about it. It is possible, sure, he said, for thermal effects to produce some small perturbation of stars; parallax effects are quite common, sure; but it would require atmospheric temperatures into the thousands of degrees to produce a show like the Midwest flap, and of course we'd all then be too fried to notice.

But the psychological espousers eat it up. I still hear this thermal inversion theory advanced to debunk hard-to-debunk reports of aerial phenomena.

The so-called Condon Report, a supposedly scientific study commissioned by the United States government and rubber-stamped by the National Academy of Science, has been revealed as an out-and-out con job on the American public, who funded that study. Condon, a professor at the University of Colorado, obviously set out in the beginning to ridicule the whole thing and succeeded in doing so by concentrating his conclusions on the most ridiculous reports he could find while ignoring the baffling ones or disposing of them under such tags as "anomalous propagation," his way of explaining away radar contacts.

The reasoning goes something like this:

a) All UFO reports are produced by deluded individuals who believe they have seen something that could not exist, or by pranksters or charlatans;

b) Objects that have no physical existence obviously cannot be detected by radar;

c) Radar has been known to display targets when no physical targets are present, the result of anomalous propagation of the radar signals;

d) Therefore any alleged radar contact suggesting impossible flight characteristics of a physical object is the result of anomalous propagation.

It does not seem to matter if the anomalous blips are describing the same aerial movements as those sighted with the naked eye by hundreds of reliable witnesses, including base commanders, fighter pilots, and other trained professionals, but the debunkers eat it up. That's okay. Let them. Just be aware that I am paying no homage to such people when I mention a possible psychological content to some of the things that I have experienced. Actually I would be surprised if there were *no* psychological content because a lot of this stuff is simply too bizarre for the human mind to handle in raw form. So we probably do "process" it just a bit in the attempt to assimilate something essentially alien to our mental models of reality.

I mean, even my mental models, which have been expanded quite a bit through the years to accommodate all manner of bizarre experiences, were taking quite a beating. Please be aware of that. I am trying to give you the real thing here. But I can give you only what is real to me.

I have to confess that I was only slightly more than half convinced of the reality of any of it as I left my car for the second time that morning and retraced my steps onto the Laker estate. And now it is time to give you a feeling for the neighborhood. It is in that section of Brentwood that is most exclusive and most seclusive, above Sunset Boulevard in canyon country. It probably would not conform to your idea of a Los Angeles neighborhood. In fact it is pretty wild up there, a jumble of canyons and serpentine roads and country lanes; it can get very rugged in spots.

Penny Laker had chosen one of those latter in which to plant her California roots. There were few neighboring structures; none at all close enough to feel really neighborly about. I guess she had several acres but only a third of it was flat enough for any practical use and the house itself took up quite a bit of that. The road was blacktopped but narrow and winding; it dead-ended about a quarter of a mile beyond the Laker place and there were no more than three or four houses on that stretch.

The atmosphere up there was still quite misty but the base of the coastal layer was now too high to discern in the darkness and the surface visibility was okay except for occasional small pockets of drifting fog.

I went back through the carport and again scaled the wall to drop into the backyard. The lanai was still lighted but the pool was not and there was no sign of my two new friends from another reality. I walked all the way around the pool looking for them. Dolphins are required to surface for air every few minutes, so I figured they'd have to show themselves pretty soon even if they were now feeling shy, but a ten-minute vigil at poolside did not reveal so much as a ripple on the surface—so if they were in there and breathing air like all the dolphins I know, they were being very quiet about it. I was wondering why they were evading me, knowing they could do so in the darkness with stealthy movements—and wondering also why I could not reestablish telepathic communication with them. But of course I was also wondering with the other half of my mind if there ever had been any dolphins in that pool and if I had somehow hallucinated the whole thing.

But the new pool was still there and it was even harder to accept than the presence of dolphins within it. On an impulse I knelt beside it and gathered a sample of the water in my hands and tasted it. It was salt water. From the Pacific?—no less than three miles distant, as the crow flies? Or was it being processed somehow from the freshwater supply?

I went looking for the answer to the salt water and found more than that. From the moment the question was raised, it became evident that I had overlooked an even more basic question: Where was the filtration system? None of the usual stuff was in evidence—pumps, pipes, filters, none of that. I found it in an underground vault beneath a manhole cover that was emplaced twenty feet behind the pool. A circular steel ladder dropped me into the vault at the same level as the bottom of the pool. I knew that because I could see the pool from down there, or at least a goodly portion of it, and nothing was separating me from it but a wall of glass.

The vault itself was maybe twenty by forty feet and it was crammed with equipment and pipes.

A series of perpendicular glass tubes about three feet in diameter were attached to the glass wall, or maybe they were part of the wall because they were filled with water except for a small air space at the top.

There were ten of those, and there were tubes and wires and other umbilicallike devices running from each of them to various items of equipment.

There was a dolphin in each one. They looked dead, but I knew that they were not.

They were, I surmised, being prepared for their new reality . . . whatever that may be.

CHAPTER NINETEEN

A Question of Time

I later learned that two new items had been added that morning to the bulging file of "crackpot" UFO lore. A commercial fisherman out of Morro Bay and two of his crewmen shamefacedly reported to the Coast Guard an incident involving their boat two miles off the California coast. All three requested polygraph tests as verification of their report, but the news item indicated that their story was not taken seriously enough to warrant any attempts at verification.

According to the skipper, his boat was dragging a sea anchor in heavy fog, all his navigation lights were showing, and he was sounding the required fog warning signals while the craft stood dead in the water, when a cement swimming pool filled with water and complete with diving board and slide descended slowly from the overcast directly above them and settled into the ocean beside their boat without a splash, as he and his crew gaped from the deck.

Little wonder, is it, that nobody thought it necessary to hook these guys up to a lie detector—except maybe the seamen who filed the other "crackpot" story. In roughly that same time frame and less than fifty miles removed from the scene of the other report, two crewmen of an oil tanker proceeding toward Santa Barbara reported seeing a vertical column of water rising from the surface of the ocean and disappearing into the low overcast. Both men emphatically insisted that they saw several dolphins swimming *up* the column of water.

Those two reports were among the most laughable to be seized upon by the press during the California flap.

I did not laugh when I read them.

In fact, I would have paid hard money for those reports if they'd come to me at the time. Because the stuff was really beginning to pile up around my ears, and the more I experienced the more I wondered about my mental health.

This new "pool" in Penny Laker's backyard was obviously a scientific laboratory of some sort. The "equipment" in that vault was definitely alien technology unrelatable to anything in my experience—various cylindrical-shaped objects of shiny metal, some larger than me, others as small as a softball—piping made of some kind of very hard but not metallic material—spaghettilike bundles of stuff that could be wiring or anything.

I could see nothing that would make me think of direct-read dials or gauges but a large panel emplaced on the far wall could conceivably be a control panel. It had "eyes" in it shaped like Donovan's, many of them, and I convinced myself that I could see subtle movements deep within them.

The dolphins looked like ordinary terrestrials to me. But if they were alive, they were in a comatose or suspended state; they were absolutely motionless; they could have been wax figures.

Each was six or seven feet long, obviously adult; I could not determine sex.

That section of the pool visible through the glass wall was apparently recessed from the main area and not visible from above because I had seen nothing earlier to suggest such a setup below.

I was trying to get a better look at the comatose dolphins when Donovan's voice spoke to me from the panel I mentioned earlier.

"They are quite healthy, Ashton."

I turned slowly to gaze at the panel, which stood about twenty feet away. "Glad to hear that," I replied. "Maybe you should tell them that."

I had already begun moving toward the panel and I was trying to home in on the precise source of the voice as Donovan responded to my little gibe, but it was a futile attempt. The voice was just "there" somewhere, evidently issuing from behind the panel yet clear and distinct. "We would not interfere in any life process without permission."

I said, speaking to the panel at large, "That's nice to know. Now how about defining 'we' for me."

There was a trace of amusement in the response. "Would you understand if I told you?"

"I'll sure try," I promised.

Then I *saw* him...in the panel, through the panel, somewhere...as through a glass darkly, just from the chin up. He was smiling as he said, "In good time, my friend. For now, just try to stay out of trouble. Will you do that?"

I was a bit irked by the tone, that of a father chastising a small boy. I said, "You know, Donovan, you've got a hell of a nerve. I don't know what you guys have in mind for this planet but I have to tell you that your methods don't always make a lot of sense. I presume there is some universal standard for good sense."

He was still having subtle fun with me as he replied, "Which universe?"

I growled, "How many are there?"

"How many would you like?" he asked.

I said, "See? You're treating me like a puppy."

The face and voice became very sober as he replied to that. "I beg your forgiveness. You are entirely correct. Superior technology does not necessarily equate to superior wisdom, does it. Take the dolphin."

I said, "Yes?"

"He is very old and very wise. Yet your superior technology allows you to exterminate him to the point of genocide. *I* have the nerve, Ashton? I have not slaughtered you, my friend. Yet you have reduced virtually every life-form upon the planet to serve your comfort. If you cannot eat it or skin it or otherwise process it for your comfort, then you exterminate it. How say you now?"

I replied, "I was about to say that I do none of that. But I guess I do, in many subtle ways."

Donovan said, "And in some ways not so subtle. But it is our fault, not yours. We brought you here and abandoned you here to shift for yourself, charging you only to subdue the planet. It appears that you have very nearly succeeded in that."

I was beginning to get a sick feeling at the pit of my stomach. I said, "Do I stand indicted for the entire race?"

He showed me a sober smile and replied, "There is no indictment, Ashton. But yes, you do answer for the race. Each of you do. How else could it be? Are you not now the heir of all that ever was before you? If you would reap the inheritance, would you not also settle the debts against the estate?"

It was getting *heavy* and my belly was having a hard time with it. I said to Donovan, "If I am the heir then who was my father?"

"I was," he replied quietly.

"Then we stand at the bar together," I told him.

"Yes," he said. "Very good. You go to the heart, don't you, my friend."

"When did you conceive me?" I asked him.

He stared at me for a moment before replying: "As you calculate time you are bound by time."

"I asked you a direct question."

"So you did. Then try nine hundred thousand terrestrial years for fit."

I said, "Neither of us is that old."

"Oh but we are, and I much older. We are older than your star, my brother; older than my present star; and there were stars before those. Time, Ashton, has no meaning to you and me. Time is an illusion produced by matter defining space. We are older than matter, brother; older than space."

"Then why can't I remember it?"

"How would you use the memory? How could you cope with it? In your present limited form, how would you *bear* it?"

I said, "Uh...we had a guy here...name was Nietzsche. He said there were no gods, otherwise how could he *bear* to be no god. Is that sort of what...?"

Donovan replied, "Very good, yes."

"You are God, then?"

He chuckled. *"We* are, yes."

I said, despairingly, "Oh shit."

Were these, then, the guys who threw the lightning bolts from Mount Olympus?—the ones who settled on Moses's mountaintop with fire and thunderings?—the same ones who inspired all the god legends across the planet?

And was it their time once again?

Time to do what?

I was not to have a direct answer at that moment. Donovan's face disappeared from view and a purplish smoke replaced it, drifted toward me, buckled my knees, dropped my chin to my chest, toppled me onto the floor, closed my eyes and my ears and all of my senses.

The last thought to flare through that darkness was from me and to me.

Was it time to pay the debts of the estate?

CHAPTER TWENTY

Echo the Stars

I looked it up later. I was not really aware until then that dolphins are actually a type of whale, most closely related to the so-called killer whale. Our experts regard the whale as a very ancient order of the mammalian class that branched off into a marine species very early in the evolutionary history of mammals, long before man appeared.

That is what our experts say. They also say that mammals first appeared on earth less than a hundred million years ago—the whales about seventy million years ago and man only one million.

We are talking large slices of time here, pal. To personalize it and bring it down to ruler size, think of yourself as all humanity from the beginning and you are a mere infant, only about a year old, while your cousin the dolphin is a great-grandpappy, seventy years old.

I gathered that this was what Donovan had reference to in comparing man and dolphin. To carry the comparison a step farther, these same experts tell us that the evolution of life on this planet began about three billion years ago —that is three thousand millions—so place the blue-green algae on your ruler at age three thousand.

On the scale of life on earth, then, our year-old babe is riding high on the crest of genetic material that had been cooking for three thousand years to produce him. But that ruler is now a distortion, as applied to genetics, because the very first cell to appear on earth was composed of potentially immortal material and traces of it are present in every gene alive on the planet today. So our babe may have a prefrontal life of only a single year but it required three thousand years of constant stewing to produce the recipe for that life.

I believe this is more or less what Donovan had in mind when he was talking about the heirs to the estate. Our endowment is that gene pool. It took a very long time to build it. Some debts were incurred along the way.

So what is the human debt to the planet and how do we repay it?

Donovan had been speaking figuratively, of course, when he said that he begat me—but there had been a literal ring to his words when he was alluding to the origins and age of mankind, the meaninglessness of time, and the common bonds between us.

As for that debt . . . well, I was to be reminded that bills come around from time to time and have to be paid from time to time if you do not want to have a valuable possession repossessed.

Maybe the mortgage had come due on Planet Earth.

I had about ten million questions to ask Donovan but I probably would not have thought of one of them even had the purple smoke not detached me from the process. I don't know, maybe I did get a few questions in somewhere because I came out of that purple haze with a vague, dreamlike memory of another conversation with Donovan while standing on a balcony in a huge domed enclosure and looking down upon hundreds of uniformed people engaged in various tasks.

In the dream or whatever, I asked him, "When do you go home?"—and he replied: "We are home now."

I think also I asked about my earlier experience when I walked into the fog and met Ambudala, because I remember the smile on Donovan's face as he struggled to convey an understanding of multidimensional reality.

"Picture a bar magnet," he suggested, "and add to the picture the electromagnetic lines of force that you know surround the magnet even though you cannot see them with the eye. Now imagine that the magnet itself is transparent and that you can see the same lines of force not only surrounding the magnet but permeating it. Fit a powerful microscope to the eye, now, and zoom in on the molecular reality. Note how each molecule dances to the lines of force and how every atom within the molecule contributes to the dance. Now go even deeper and watch the particles of an atom as they give to and take from the rhythm of the dance. Hold that focus but gradually enlarge the field of vision until you are seeing the entire bar magnet as individual particles moving within those same lines of force—and now tell me, Ashton, what your magnet looks like."

I had the image in my mind. I told him, "The same particles define both. It just seems to move more slowly and more densely when defining the bar itself."

"Exactly," he responded. "There is your reality, my brother."

I said, "It's all in the vibrations."

"It could be so simplified, yes, one field meshing with another and another, on and on infinitely, and the scale is also infinite. What is music, Ashton, but a scale within which dance the tones and harmonics of particles in motion? But is the tune mere particles in motion or is it a synthesis of overlapping fields vibrating from the mind of the composer through the mind of the musician to the mind of the listener, and do these fields not guide the particles along their dance? When you hear Beethoven, does your very brain not vibrate as his did when he composed the piece? Is music not multidimensional? Is the bar magnet not? Are you not?"

I commented, "Experience itself, then, is a matter of being tuned to a particular wavelength. There are some wavelengths I can't tune to. If I had an infinite tuner..."

"You're on the right track, yes. But you need to refine it. And perhaps you need to redefine experience. Experience is but the echo, my friend."

"Echo of what?"

He smiled and told me, "When you understand that, then you will understand all."

But, as a matter of fact, I understood nothing. I awoke to that realization, and to a feeling of utter frailty, total helplessness, and complete despair.

So I guess I saw a lot more in that "dream" than I consciously remembered. Because I felt like a smudge of blue-green algae.

* * *

The sun was in the sky when I awoke and I was lying on a chaise on Penny Laker's lanai. I was fully clothed, shoes and all, and held an unlit cigarette between my fingers. I guess I vocalized something as I sat up, because I drew the immediate attention of two concerned women. Both were wearing string bikinis and nothing else. Penny stepped over from the pool area. She had obviously been in the water recently. Julie came from the kitchen carrying a tray with orange juice and coffee. She put the tray on the table, then both of them just stood there staring at me with quizzical gazes.

I noted for the first time how alike they looked, standing side by side and practically naked. Same height, same body contours, same soft and smooth-all-over femininity, except that Penny was blond and Julie raven-haired. You would not even read that much difference in age, though there had to be some ten to fifteen years between them.

This seemed like the Penny Laker I had known for the past few years. I'm speaking of the personality and mannerisms. But she was not exactly hospitable. She seemed puzzled by my presence there, too proper to demand an explanation but also probably just a bit upset about the whole thing.

We were acquaintances more than friends, understand, but I still thought she was acting peculiarly under the circumstances. I mean, okay, I'd just dropped in without an invitation but we were involved in a common puzzle and I had done the lady a couple of good turns in recent hours. She was looking at me as though wondering how to handle a gate-crashing fan.

Julie's behavior was even more puzzling. She turned around without a word and snared a terry-cloth robe from the back of a chair, put it on, went back inside the house.

I went to the table and helped myself to the coffee, told Penny, "Sorry to crash in on you this way. Well, no, actually I am not sorry because I did not crash in. I think Donovan dropped me here. You know? Donovan? The guy in the silver BVD's?"

She showed me a thoughtful smile and a shake of the head as she replied, "No, I...I'm sorry, Ashton, you startled me. I didn't see you come in, and..."

I said, "Okay, so maybe he beamed me here. I don't recall arriving, myself." I looked her up and down. "I see you've been in the pool. Enjoy the dolphins?"

Her smile grew even more puzzled but it hung on as she replied, "Yes, I love dolphins. Don't you?" She did not give me a chance to respond to that but hurried on with: "Ashton, I must ask you to excuse me. I have a very busy schedule today and—what can I do for you?"

I sipped the hot coffee while intently studying her over the rim of the cup. She was a superb actress, sure, but I could not read this as an act.

I put the coffee down, showed her a smile, said, "Don't let me detain you. Actually I'm looking for Ted."

"Isn't he at his office?"

"Not today," I told her.

The actress sat down across from me with a searching gaze. I was visualizing her in the silver uniform as she asked me, in a concerned voice, "Are you all right, Ashton?"

I said, "Probably not. But why do you ask?"

"Well... you came in here yelling 'What planet is this?' and you really haven't said anything more sensible than that since you arrived. Are you drunk? Would you like to sleep it off?"

I did not respond to any of that. "Do you like your new pool?"

"I love it, yes. How'd you know about that? Did Ted tell you? Oh! Oh! I get it!" She looked around expectantly. "Where is he? How did he *ever* pull it off?"

I growled, "Relax, Ted's not here. He's in Buenos Aires, or at some point in transit."

I left her sitting at the table with a dumb look on her face and crossed to the far side of the pool. It was the new pool, yeah, but I could not find the manhole cover. I even got on my hands and knees and covered the entire surrounding area with probing fingers but I could not find it. Penny was watching from the other side and pacing nervously, as though undecided as to what she should do.

I stripped down to my jockeys and went into the pool, oriented myself, then dived for the glass wall. But of course there was no glass wall down there. On the second dive I did find the evidence to preserve my sanity, a barely noticeable seam about ten feet long and three feet deep outlining what I took to be a "flap" in the side of the pool.

I carried my clothing back to the lanai, toweled dry, and got dressed without a word to my hostess nor her to me. While I was donning socks and shoes, Julie reappeared, clad in the now familiar workout suit with a shorty skirt pulled over it.

She showed me a dazzling smile; said, "I'm ready,

Ashton," then went over to say something privately to her employer.

A moment later I was leaving via the front door with a radiant Julie Marsini on my arm.

Hell, I'd decided, I was ready, too.

For most anything.

CHAPTER TWENTY-ONE

Sweet Memory of Life

Julie's mood altered drastically the moment she was in the car. She folded her legs beneath her and sat with her back to the door, all troubled and sober and groping for words. "Ashton, I...I'm scared to death and I...need to talk to...somebody about it."

I put the car in motion then tried to show her a reassuring smile. "You're in luck, kid. I just happen to be somebody."

That got a wee smile out of her but the voice was still sober and troubled. "I don't want...anybody...to think that I'm...being disloyal. To Penny, I mean. But something...something very strange is going on and...and I just don't know how to cope with it."

I sighed and showed her my own troubled self. "Tell me about it. It's been nothing but strange piled on top of strange for days now. So what do you think it's all about?"

She slowly shook her head to emphasize her own confusion as she replied, "Well either I'm crazy or..."

I prodded her gently. "Uh-huh?"

"Well I'm not crazy. Do I act crazy to you?"

I said, "No, but there's still hope that you could get as crazy as me. You're talking crazy, kid, to a guy who hears voices, sees visions, and talks with the dead. So if you're looking for sympathy..."

She showed me a wan smile. "I've heard those things about you. It's really true, then?"

So, hey, with an opening like that, this lady got the story of my life. Guess I held the floor for twenty minutes straight. Not that I am usually all that eager to unload myself onto people but because I figured she needed the contrast to her own problems. It worked. She was giggling and questioning before I even got to my days at the Pentagon, and we were warm good friends by the time I ran dry. Sex is not always the ultimate intimacy. I mean, sure, in a sense there is no other way that two people can so totally interface, but sometimes that interface produces an aftermath of cover-up and retreat that is the exact opposite of intimacy—and you can't just lie together all the time, can you.

I bring it up because that was the way I had been reading Julie's reaction to me after that crazy lovin' night at Malibu. That should have forged a closer relationship, but in fact it had not.

I had been driving aimlessly through West Los Angeles as we talked. Now it was about noontime and my belly was reminding me that I'd sent nothing down for quite a while. We started looking for a likely place and found a charming sidewalk café with a low noise level and inviting shade. The conversation resumed as we brunched, and I got the story of Julie's life as she knew it.

All she knew of her origins was that she was adopted at the age of four by Giorgio Marsini. I'd heard of the guy. Probably you have, too. He'd made quite a name for himself as a movie producer in Italy but did not do so well in Hollywood. He'd married an unknown actress shortly after arriving in the country, adopted Julie a year later, and the unknown actress took a powder a year after that. So Marsini raised the kid himself. And there were hard times, though Marsini always kept up a good front. And it seems that his home was usually well populated with "starlets" so there was always a feminine influence in young Julie's life though her father never married again. He died broke when she was eighteen. In fact, he put a gun to his head and pulled the trigger—that is how bad things were.

The resident starlet at that moment was Penny Laker, though she was then known as Penelope Powers. The movie that boosted her to fame was the same one that killed Giorgio Marsini. He'd put every nickel he could beg, borrow, and steal into the production—and the thing bombed. Penelope Powers did not, and her next outing was as Penny Laker. She took Julie Marsini with her. They'd been together ever since.

I commented, "So you've been living beneath a very big shadow."

"I've never been aware that I was in the shadows," Julie replied. "We're like sisters. We've always gotten along fine. Penny tends to be a bit disorganized. I guess I am a naturally organized person, so I've never had a problem finding a way to be useful."

I said, "Yeah, but life can't be all work and sisterhood, you know. How have you gotten along with Ted?"

"By ignoring him," she replied quietly.

"What does that mean?"

"It means he's a jerk. But Penny doesn't know that yet and I'm not going to be the one to tell her."

"The guy been hitting on you?"

She gave me a flash of eyes. "Since the honeymoon."

I sighed and commented, "It figures. Some guys just..."

Julie said, "Especially that guy. He has a dozen girls on the string all the time, and still he comes home and tries to warm my bed."

"Penny doesn't know about that."

"I hope not."

"You should tell her. That is what a friend would do. Tell her."

"I can't *do* that."

"She know about the other women?"

Julie sighed and bit her upper lip. "I don't know. Sometimes I wonder how she could *not* know. I mean, he has no finesse, and he's a jerk, and how could she help but know. I think she just chooses not to know. In all fairness, Ted is a good manager. I think she needs him because..."

"Because what?"

"Well, because she's so scattered. Especially the past year or so."

"What do you think is happening there? Why is she so scattered?"

Julie shrugged delicately. "I don't know. She's always

been . . . well, never well organized. It's just that it has gotten worse."

"A lot worse?"

"A lot worse, yes."

"Like the dolphins."

"Yes. About six months ago she met this woman who claims to have some sort of psychic connection with dolphins. Her name is Dee Townsend. About Penny's age, and—"

"What would that be?"

"Penny's age? Oh, I—you can't ask me that."

I grinned. "Okay. What about this psychic?"

"I guess she's psychic only with dolphins. At least she claims to be. She leads these groups to Zuma Beach twice a week. They sit out there and call the dolphins." She shrugged. "I guess they come because the same people keep going back and back."

"You say the name is Dee Townsend?"

"Uh-huh. I think she's quite sincere. But she's a little batty, too."

I said, "But the dolphins come."

Julie smiled. "Okay. Maybe she's not so batty."

"What kind of messages are they getting from the dolphins?"

"Peace and love and brotherhood and all the usual stuff. Dee is writing a book. So I guess there's more to it than that. But it seems mainly, what I get from Penny, just that they love us and are worried about us, and they're afraid we're going to destroy the planet. Them with it, I guess."

I said, "Uh-huh."

"Penny has joined the antinuclear group. I guess she

has donated quite a bit of money. And she goes to their rallies. You know she was arrested last month in Nevada."

I said, "No, I didn't know that."

"Uh-huh. It was a protest demonstration. They sat in the road and blocked the entry to that underground test site. The police came and hauled them away. Penny was one of those."

"What else has she been into?"

"Oh it's always something. Central America, the Middle East, whatever. Penny's always good for a few dollars and a celebrity face on television."

"Is this what you call scattered?"

"Wouldn't you? She hasn't made a picture in a year and a half."

"Ted told me that, yeah. Guess he's pretty upset about it."

"Well it's his meal ticket, isn't it."

I mildly suggested, "Maybe that's not entirely fair. It sounds to me like it has been a symbiotic relationship. They feed each other. Why shouldn't he be concerned about that?"

She said, "I guess you're right. But where is he now? —with all this going on?"

I said, "All this what?"

"You know what I mean. All this."

"The dolphins."

"Yes."

"And the swimming pool."

"Yes."

"And Donovan."

"Yes." She blinked at me, caught herself; said, "What? Who is Donovan?"

"He's the guy in the silver suit. The kind Penny was wearing last night."

"What?"

"You know what. Focus on it. Penny was wearing a uniform. It was like a workout suit except silvery metallic. Donovan wore one, too. Focus."

"I—I can't. I thought I—but it . . ."

"We were aboard the spacecraft. Penny was there. Donovan was there. Silver uniforms. Big domed room. Long ramp. Focus. We went down the ramp hand in hand and ended up on my living room floor. Focus, Julie, dammit."

"I can't."

I had to believe it, because I had been watching her eyes and reading the fuzzies in there. All she was getting were phantom fragments freezing between the synapses.

But I thought I knew how to get at it.

"Ever been hypnotized?" I asked quietly.

"No."

"Do you trust me?"

She silently debated that one for a moment, then replied, "I guess so."

"Would you like to find out for sure how crazy you are?"

"I think so."

"Let me put you in trance."

Her gaze rebounded from mine and fled to an inspection of our surroundings. Presently her eyes rested on me and she began breathing again.

"Do you know what you're doing? I mean, is it safe?"

I said, "Promise, I know what I'm doing and your consciousness will be entirely safe with me. I think it's important that we find out what is buried in your memory gaps. I'd love to find out what is buried in mine, but I don't know anyone competent who I would trust with that. You're lucky; you've got me."

She looked about her again, said in a weak voice: "Right here?"

"My place," I said.

"Oh dear," she said.

"What more could you give me at my place," I pointed out, "that you have not already given?"

She laughed quietly, took my hand, looked down at it; murmured, "Let's go find out."

CHAPTER TWENTY-TWO
Of Spoken Word

There is nothing magical or mystical about hypnosis. A lot of phenomenal stuff can happen under hypnosis, sure, but that is because the mind itself is phenomenal and hypnosis can free it up to do its thing. The hypnotic trance is simply another state of consciousness, entirely natural, during which the hypnotist directly accesses the deeper domains of the mind.

There is more to it than that, of course, and there are various levels of trance. The deeper the trance, the more phenomenal the results, but even the lightest levels of trance can produce marked alterations of personality if the therapist is patient and persistent. What that means is that eight to ten or more light-trance sessions may be required to achieve the same results that a single deep-trance session would produce. Of course I did not have time for patience and persistence, so I was hoping that Julie Marsini would prove to be a good subject for deep-trance hypnosis.

151

As it turned out, she was an excellent subject. I have worked with hypnosis quite a bit, but I can count on the fingers of one hand the number of subjects I have known to achieve the very deep somnambulistic level in the first session. In that level of trance the subject can open the eyes and walk about the room without breaking the trance, can produce startlingly strong positive and negative hallucinations, can even produce different personalities, and of course has absolute memory recall.

Julie was in a somnambulistic trance five minutes after I began the induction routines. She opened her eyes upon command—laughed, wept, sang, shivered, and shuddered upon command—altered her own heartbeat, and raised and lowered her own blood pressure upon command.

I had a hot one and I loved it. At a more relaxed time I would have paid this girl to sit for me in a research project. But the time was not relaxed, the circumstances not right for leisurely research. So I went right to work on her repressed memories. She was comfortably reclined on the old leather chair in my study, eyes open and looking at me, and if someone had walked in on that conversation there would not have been a clue as to what was actually going on there.

"Are you comfortable?"

"Oh very."

"Stay comfortable. Shift about however you'd like to remain comfortable. Remain focused on me. Any other sounds that may come into this room will only deepen your trance. You will find no distractions. Focus on me. Respond only to me. Speak only the truth, only the whole truth, and speak only to me. Do not fabricate answers for me, Julie. Do not try to please me by telling me something simply because you think I want to hear that particular thing. It will not please me, Julie, if you tell me anything but the truth. Do you understand?"

"Yes. I understand."

"What is your name?"

"My name is Julie Marsini."

"And how old are you, Julie?"

"I am—I think I am—I was told that I was four when Poppa found me. That was twenty-four years ago. So I guess I'm twenty-eight. Is that right?"

"The mathematics are right, yes. You say Poppa found you. Where did he find you?"

"I guess I was in a home."

"But you don't know for sure?"

"I don't know for sure. I was four when Poppa found me."

"How about your birth certificate? Doesn't it tell you when you were born?"

"I don't have one. I never had one. Poppa always laughed and said he found me under a rock."

"Poppa was Giorgio Marsini?"

"Yes."

"Was he nice to you?"

"Oh yes."

"You loved him."

"Oh yes, I loved him."

"Did he ever talk to you about where and how he found you?"

Julie smiled, enjoying some warm memory. "Under a rock in Never Never Land."

"Do you love Penny Laker?"

"Oh yes. We are like sisters."

"Do you like living with Penny and working with Penny?"

"Oh yes."

"There's nothing else you'd like to be doing with your life?"

"No. What else would I do?"

"You're a bright girl, a pretty girl. You could do anything you wanted to do. What do you want to do?"

"I must serve my sister."

"What? You *must* serve her?"

"Yes, I must."

"Who told you that?"

"Who told me that? Who told me that?"

"I asked you, Julie. Who told you that you must serve your sister?"

My subject was becoming agitated. I moved quickly to another question.

"It's okay, just relax, everything's okay. Tell me about the dolphins."

"Peace and love."

"Did you know that dolphins are carnivorous? They are predators."

"They eat fish, I think."

"Yes, and that makes them predators. So where is all this peace and love when the big fish is eating the little fish?"

"Well a dolphin is not a fish."

"I was speaking figuratively. Dolphins are no different than men, are they? Don't we both hunt and fish and eat flesh?"

"I guess so."

"So I guess peace and love depends upon the point of view."

"I guess so."

"How many dolphins are in your swimming pool right now?"

"Two, I think."

"How do you know that?"

"I saw two. Didn't we see two?"

"Yes, we saw two dolphins swimming in the pool. What are those dolphins eating? The ones in your pool. What are they eating?"

"I don't know."

"How did they get there?"

"I don't know."

"Who enlarged the pool?"

"I don't know."

"Did Donovan enlarge the pool and bring the dolphins?"

"Yes."

"Yes? Donovan did that?"

"Maybe he did."

"You know Donovan, then."

"I must serve my sister."

"Did Donovan tell you that?"

"No. I don't know." She was getting flustered again. "D'Ahnov'e'n." This last word came with clicks and tongue trills. I had no idea what she'd said.

"Give me that again, Julie. That last word. Say it again."

She said it the same way. I asked her to spell it. She spelled it the way I showed above. A phonetic spelling that comes close but does not duplicate the clicks and trills is: Duh-awn-ove-ee-un.

I was momentarily flustered myself.

"That is Donovan?"

"I think so, yes."

"Okay. Let's take it back to the very first time you saw or met with Donovan. Drift back to that point in time, your first meeting with Donovan. Now tell me about it."

"Uh, forbidden, I cannot."

"No, I think you can. Someone has programmed you, Julie. Now we're going to de-program. I want you to tell me about your very first meeting with Donovan."

"I cannot."

"Was Penny there?" I had encountered a block, and I was trying to get around it.

"Penny is always there."

"Can you see her uniform?"

"Yes."

"Can you describe it for me?"

"Yes. It is like silver lamé. It fits very closely like a bodysuit."

"What is Penny's name when she is wearing the uniform?"

"Her name is Penny."

"What is her other name, her *real* name?"

"She is Penny. Penny loves me. I will serve my sister."

"Clear to the grave, eh?"

"Till it is time."

"Time for what?"

"Time for the change."

"What change?"

"You know...change, metamorphosis, the new world."

"Where is the new world?"

"I don't know. Return. It will return."

"Return from where?"

"From the depths, from the slumber."

"Where are the depths? Where is the new world slumbering?"

"Pyramid."

"Pyramid? What does that mean, Julie? Tell me what pyramid means to you."

"Promise. We shall return."

"Try triangle. What does the triangle mean?"

"Trine. Holy trinity. Union. The triangle is perfection. It is father, son, and holy ghost. It is three gathered together in my name. It is..."

"Go on. What else does the triangle mean?"

I immediately wished I hadn't asked that. Because Julie began talking a streak in that other tongue, the click-and-trill language, and I did not get her back again until I terminated the trance.

I later dubbed that part of the tape and took it to a language expert at UCLA. He thought I was playing a joke on him, wanted to know how I'd managed to get an African Bushman and a dolphin at the same microphone at the same time. I just let it go at that because I knew the guy couldn't help me anyway.

As for Julie and that first trance session, I thought it best to keep the wraps on for the moment, so I brought her back with no memory of the trance. She looked at me with a smile and said, "Didn't work, huh?"

"We'll do better next time," I assured her.

"When will we try again?"

"Later tonight, maybe," I replied.

"Oh. Well. How will we ever fill the time between now and then?"

But of course she knew how. We both knew how.

Time *is* relative, you see. It can be a burden or a joy, a trial or a celebration.

We both opted for joyful celebration, which is what loving should always be. Even and especially with the new world a-dawning, and D'Ahnov'e'n waiting in the wings to cart the old one away.

CHAPTER TWENTY-THREE

Tagged and Bagged

If you keep up with the UFO stuff then you probably already know that many people who experience so-called encounters of the third kind—usually an abduction experience—have very little conscious memory of the encounter until the echoes of it begin to plague their dreams or until they seek therapy for a mental disturbance caused by the encounter. Hypnosis is usually employed in the latter case, the victims regressed, and the story extracted from their subconscious, such as in the highly publicized case of the New England couple, Betty and Barney Hill. The Hill case has become a textbook example of such encounters, in which the victims usually remember seeing a UFO and then report a discontinuity of experience, sometimes with a memory gap of many hours.

Under hypnotic regression, they then relate a terrifying story of capture by strange beings who subject them to medical examinations but otherwise treat them kindly and let them go.

For a close parallel with a better yardstick, try to put yourself inside the hide of an endangered animal such as a bear or mountain goat in the American West who is chased down by a helicopter and shot with a tranquilizer gun by an animal conservation team, then either tagged for future tracking or airlifted to a better feeding area.

How do you describe the experience to your friends? More than that, how do you explain it to yourself?

A human is surely in every respect as much or more an alien to a mountain goat as visitors from the Pleiades are to us. Don't try to tell the mountain goat where Denver is located, certainly not Los Angeles, and don't expect him ever to understand why these strange creatures who walk upright on their hind legs swoop down from the skies to abduct him, stick sharp objects into him or attach strange devices to him, then let him go.

Of course we can find an even closer parallel. Roll it back a few thousand or even a few hundred years with a time machine and go exploring with a Land Rover, see what kind of stories are developed by intelligent human beings of that time frame who encounter you during your explorations.

To get an idea, though, of just how close to us—how much like us—are these modern aliens in their terrifying flying machines, consider the human world of just two hundred years ago and check how far we have advanced technologically in that short span of time. You've turned the clock back in just two centuries to the time before railroads or steamships, before radio or the telegraph, before vaccinations or blood transfusions or even anesthesia. *That* is the more alien world to people of today. Space travel and supersonic transportation—radio and television and global communications networks—organ transplants and test-tube babies—automobiles and freeways and subways and skyscrapers—*there* is the alien world to men like Ben Franklin or Thomas Jefferson, neither of whom could have accommodated a mental model of our world from their viewpoint of a mere two hundred years ago.

So what if the Pleiadians are a couple of hundred years more advanced than us. That does not make them gods. If our technological pace of only the past fifty years continues into the year 2200 A.D., how quaint will our world of today seem to our descendants?

So I find it very strange that men and women today speak from our halls of science in such limiting terms, who ridicule *without even investigating* any report of visitors from other worlds, who use our own infantile understanding of science and technology as a yardstick to measure the limitations of older worlds than ours.

Isaac Newton could have had no mental model of the Concorde SST or even a Piper Cub. In his wildest fantasies he could not have concocted a vision of today's La Guardia Airport or the launchpads at Cape Kennedy—not even the automobile or express elevator or the Empire State building—motion pictures?—television?—Yankee Stadium?—how about a vacuum cleaner, when he did not even know electricity?

Does the average person today really understand how far we have come in just the past century? Or how about just the past sixty years, the beginning of which marked Lindbergh's heroic flight across the Atlantic?

So what about Julie Marsini's "new world" and what could that signify?

Could it mean that Planet Earth is about to become a member of the intergalactic community of enlightened worlds?

Or were we going to be chastised and demoted and sent back to try to learn it right next time?

I had never been a doomsdayer and I had never feared new ideas, new ways, new growth. I saw no reason to begin that now. And Donovan had really given me no reason to fear him. Quite the opposite, he had shown me every reason to trust him. God or whatever, I liked the guy. I just wished that I could get over the nagging worry that maybe we were no more than a laboratory planet, and that these guys were coming back to try some new experiments on us.

I did not want to be relocated, like the mountain goat, to a new feeding ground even though a better one, nor did I wish to be tagged and tracked and monitored for the rest of my small life on this obscure planet.

Hell, they already had me tagged.

There was a new star in the heavens directly above my house. I spotted it at first dark. And then I went back to Julie for another go at total recall, muttering to myself, "God help us all."

I did not want a repetition of the conclusion to the first trance so this time I devoted a few preliminary minutes to the proper conditioning of my subject. I worked in some posthypnotic codes that would greatly shorten the induction routines in any future sessions, then I built in some controls to strengthen my own influence while she was in trance.

"You will hear and respond only to my voice."

"Okay."

"If any other voice attempts to speak to you, any voice other than my own, you will immediately awaken. Understand? Any other voice speaking to you will immediately break the trance."

"I understand."

"You will then immediately return to trance when I tell you to. I will place my hand on your forehead and I will say, 'Go back, Julie.' You will then return to the deepest trance level and you will be responsive only to my voice."

"Okay. I understand."

"You will speak to me only in the English language. No other tongues. Understand?"

"Yes."

"Fine. Stay comfortable. When did you first meet Donovan?"

"Long ago."

"How long ago?"

Julie fidgeted a bit, snapped her eyes at me, replied: "Not sure. Long ago."

It can be a bit unnerving sometimes to work with a subject's eyes open and expressive—and of course not every subject can remain in trance with the eyes open—but I have found that mode much more productive if it can be achieved. Eyes can speak volumes with no help whatever from the voice.

There were barriers around Donovan in Julie's consciousness, perhaps very carefully constructed barriers. I did not want to push too hard against those defenses. There are better ways.

"When did you first meet Penny Laker?"

"Penelope Powers."

"What?"

"You said you wanted her other name."

"That was last time, Julie. You are carrying over from the first trance. I want to leave the first trance behind us for now. Okay?"

"Okay."

"So when did you first meet Penny or Penelope?"

"Long ago."

"When you were about eighteen? Or before that?"

"Before that."

"I want you to let go of present time and space. Drift back, back through the years to your first meeting with Penny and I—"

"Let's use Penelope. I can talk about Penelope."

See? Even in trance, the mind is fully there. Sometimes a subject will help you find a way around a memory block.

"Fine. That's good. I want to talk about Penelope. We're floating back to your first meeting. Tell me when you are there."

"Okay. I can see her."

Julie's voice changed subtly as she said that, became almost childlike. This is common in regression experiences. Sometimes that is good and sometimes it is not, as you shall see.

"What is Penelope wearing?"

A very tiny and immature voice responded, "Angel."

"She is an angel?"

She clapped her hands together and squealed delightedly, heaving upright and grasping her ankles in both hands and staring with fascinated eyes at some phantom scene projected from the mind.

"Stay with me, Julie. Stay out of the scene. How is Penelope dressed?"

That same tiny voice squealed, "Shiny! Angel!"

"How old are you, Julie?"

She held up three fingers for me to see but did not otherwise respond.

"Okay, we're coming out of there but we're bringing the scene with us. Moving forward as I speak. Four years old, five, ten, fifteen years old and back to the present but bring the memory with you. How was Penelope dressed?"

Julie turned puzzled eyes to me. "I—Ashton? Am I awake or asleep?"

I looked at her closely and asked her, "Why did you awaken?"

"I don't know."

"Do you remember what you awakened from?"

"No."

"So okay, we're going back. On the numbers, the way we did it before. Deep sleep again by the time we reach five. One...two...three...four...five and deeply asleep, back where we were when you woke up. Why did you wake up, Julie?"

"Someone talked to me."

"Who talked to you?"

"Not you."

"I understand that. And I told you that you would awaken if someone else spoke to you. Who spoke to you?"

"Ashton?"

I put a hand to her forehead and commanded, "Go

back, Julie. Back to the depths, very deep. Are you okay?"

"I'm fine."

"Who spoke to you?"

"Dammit, Ashton! What is going on here?"

It was that quick, from deep trance to full wakefulness each time I touched that barrier.

I sighed, lit a cigarette, told my bewildered subject, "Sorry, kid. I've no right to jerk you around like that. Let's take a break then try again."

Hell, we had to try again. And I had to figure a way to outwit the gods in the struggle for this woman's memory. Something was locked up in there, that was certain. But this was a human mind, not a computer, and I could not hack my way in there. Suddenly I realized that I'd gone about it all wrong. I was playing the game backward.

I did not need to outwit the gods.

I just needed to get in touch with them.

CHAPTER TWENTY-FOUR

Frames of Reality

"Are you comfortable, Julie?"

"Yes."

"Stay that way. Listen very closely, now. What I said earlier about waking up if you hear other voices, I am now canceling that. That no longer applies. Here is what I want you to do instead. Listen closely. I am your guide here. No one else may guide you but me. If other voices come to you, let them in and let them through, let them speak to me, and we will insist that they speak to me in the English language. Do you understand?"

"I understand."

"Who is Penelope Powers?"

"She is my sister and I serve her."

"What are you called?"

"I am called Julie Marsini."

"Have you ever been called anything else?"

"Yes, I think so."

167

"What name have you been called, other than Julie Marsini?"

"I believe . . . I have been called . . ."

"Yes? Give me the name."

It came with a trill and a click and it sounded like "Luh-ill-ro-too."

"Thank you. You told me yesterday that you thought you had been awakened by the visitors. What did you mean by that?"

"My true self awakened."

"I see. And your true self is Luh-ill-ro-too?"

"Yes, I think so."

"But you are a native of earth."

"No."

"No? Where, then?"

"Another world. I don't know the name. I was brought here when I was very young."

"Who brought you?"

"Angels brought me. And Poppa found me under a rock in Never Never Land."

"Aren't you a bit confused, Julie? Who told you that angels brought you here?"

"Poppa told me."

"I see. Wasn't this just a fantasy? The kind a father would use to explain to his little girl where babies come from?"

"I saw the angels."

"You saw them? When?"

"Many times."

"You mean when you were a little girl."

"Yes."

"What did these angels look like?"

went out to the pool. Things were very quiet out there. I again searched for the manhole cover and again could not find it. I decided that they had either moved the operation or moved the access to it. I hung around out there for about five minutes, thinking maybe I would get another telepathic contact but I did not.

There was about an hour and a half to kill before I would have to leave for LAX to pick up Bransen. All was definitely quiet at the Laker mansion, however, and I could see no point to hanging around there, so I drove down to Wilshire and found an all-night coffee shop, ordered coffee and took it to the pay phone, tried my luck on some long shots.

Grover Dalton, the deputy sheriff who'd come to UFO grief, had been discharged from the hospital.

My friend the Associated Press stringer did not answer either of his telephones.

Ditto for my other friend at the radio station.

So I bought a *Times* from the newspaper box and took it to the table with my coffee. That is when I learned of the two marine incidents involving dolphins in the sky and a swimming pool in the ocean. Such a simple solution, when you've got that kind of power; that was my reaction, anyway. Then it reached my funny bone and I chuckled through a further futile search for other UFO reports. It seemed that the gods did not command much newspaper space in Los Angeles—and what the hell, it's the City of Angels.

Not funny, no, but at least I was recovering my sense of humor about the whole thing. I wondered if Deputy Dalton had recovered his. No need to wonder about Ted

CHAPTER TWENTY-FIVE

Noteworthy

Julie and I shared a quiet supper at my place, then I took her home. It was about ten o'clock when I pulled into the Laker driveway. I wanted to talk to Penny, but Julie thought it could wait until morning. We compromised by agreeing that I could talk to her if she'd not yet gone to bed, otherwise it would wait.

Turned out to be a waste of argument because Penny was not even at home. The houseman did not know where she'd gone and there was no note, which disturbed Julie very much. There was a message from Ted Bransen, though, and that disturbed Julie even more.

She told me, "He's arriving on American at twelve-thirty and wants to be picked up. That means I have to drive down to LAX tonight."

So I volunteered my services. Wanted to talk to the guy, anyway. Julie was physically and emotionally exhausted so I did not have to offer twice. She kissed me and went off to bed. I turned on all the patio lights and ically beam specific control instructions to individuals in the governments and armed forces.

If these guys actually thought of themselves as *gods* . . .

So maybe they were. A god, to qualify for the title, should be omnipotent, omniscient, and omnipresent. Did these guys qualify?

I didn't know.

I just did not know.

And I decided that I really did not want to know.

symptoms of heat prostration and dehydration because you told him that he is lost in the middle of the Sahara.

He will obligingly develop a rash if you tell him he has measles and he may even remove all of his clothing in public if you tell him it is a nudist camp.

These are examples of positive hallucination and autonomic confusion.

The negatives are just as dramatic. Tell your subject at the theater that he is alone in the building; he will not hear the music or see the actors or otherwise be aware of any human presence.

A subject who normally experiences an allergic reaction to cats will sit quite comfortably in a room crawling with cats if you have told him that no animals are present.

I once participated in an experiment in which a male subject was given a posthypnotic suggestion that all the women in the world would become invisible every day between the hours of noon and five o'clock; the PH had to be removed the next day because the subject was crashing into his female employees while frantically searching for them, and it was feared that he might run someone down in his car if allowed to leave the office with the PH intact.

All of these effects can be produced by amateurs experimenting with how-to books on hypnosis. It can be very dangerous in irresponsible hands.

But consider how dangerous it could be in expert and willful hands when the intent is to disable and dominate.

I was considering the danger of hostile alien telepaths who perhaps could *broadcast* such illusions to an unsuspecting populace. They could even conceivably telepath-

"I think," I told her, "that Luh-ill-ro-too was something like a dolphin."

"Gee, thanks." That verbal response was sarcastic, but the shiver in the eyes as it was delivered was not. And neither was mine.

The telepathic relay with Donovan was not particularly enlightening, but at least it provided some mental clues to work with. First of all it confirmed an old belief that the saucer people were telepaths and secondly that some form of mind control explained the mental trauma of some contactees.

Just put those two facts together and they are enough to shiver you, if you think about it. Forget super-sophisticated weaponry and saucer razzle-dazzle; if those people could produce mass psychic effects at long range through sheer power of the mind, what other weaponry would be required?

Any effect that can be produced through hypnosis can be produced by any direct avenue into the subconscious. So if those guys could directly access your subconscious telepathically then they could manipulate your reality in any way that suited them. You tell a hypnotized subject in deep trance that a grizzly bear just walked into the room and that subject will not only see and hear a bear, he will smell it and even be able to touch it and to feel it touching him, and he could even die from terror. That is the power of the subconscious mind.

Tell the same subject that the temperature just dropped forty degrees and he will shiver and turn blue. Or he can be sitting in an air-conditioned office yet suffering all the tiny. All your questions resolve to that focus. Keep it there. We will come for you when it is time."

"Time for what?"

"Ashton?"

"Goddammit! Time for *what*, Donovan?"

"Ashton! There's no one here but you and me!"

Yeah. He'd dumped Julie out of her trance. I put her back under only to bring her out again in a proper way. Then we went out on the deck to commune with the heavens.

Many worlds, yes.

Many more worlds than the naked eye could see or the human mind could imagine.

And D'Ahnov'e'n's mobile world was still up there, shining down on us. I idly wondered if ATC and NORAD were picking up anomalous propagation blips on their radars, and which celestial mirage the astronomers were advancing to explain that world to the press.

Linked destiny, huh?

Okay. I'd buy it. I knew that we could do a whole lot worse.

I told Julie, "I talked to Donovan. He came through you while you were in trance. Do you remember Luh-ill-ro-too?"

She gave me a murky gaze and shook her head in a negative response.

I said, "You are not an alien. Not now. But I believe you were in a previous life, and your name then was Luh-ill-ro-too. That's not at all familiar to you?"

She shivered as she replied, "No, but the sound of it gives me goose bumps."

"Yes. Can we talk about that?"

"I cannot volunteer information. But if you ask, I will try to answer."

"What is going on here, Donovan?"

"Oh, that's much too general. You'll have to get more specific."

"When I walked through your fog this morning, did I hallucinate or was I actually in another world for a while?"

"You did not hallucinate."

"Where was I?"

"Ashton, there are many worlds. Be content to know that you visited one of them. You would not understand more than that."

"I resent that all to hell, Donovan. Don't presume what I will and will not understand."

"Very well." The rest of the statement came as a series of trills and clicks.

"Not funny, brother. Translate that for me, please."

"You have no language for what has not been experienced or imagined."

"I have language for purple skies, bottomless canals, and dolphins with human faces. Just fill in the blanks for me, please."

"You can do that for yourself."

"Who are you, D'Ahnov'e'n? What is your business with the human race? Why was Penny alone and naked in the night and why did you send her husband to South America? What is this new world you guys are pushing and how will it affect human destiny? What—?"

"Ah but you see, my brother, your destiny is our des-

"Very beautiful. Shining. They came at night and woke me up and we talked."

"I see. Did any of them look like Penny?"

"I think so. I think Penny is one of them."

"Like Donovan?"

"D'Ahnov'e'n, yes."

"Let's talk about D'Ahnov'e'n."

"Okay."

"I know that he is listening to us at this moment. He is here with us. Isn't he?"

"I am here, Ashton." It was Julie's vocal cords but the precision elocution was pure Donovan.

"I will talk to Donovan now, Julie. Stay close by, and come back when I tell you to. Thank you for coming, Donovan. I hope I am not disappointing you, but I feel that I must get to the bottom of this."

"You have not disappointed us, Ashton. Why do you think we selected you? So that you would do nothing?"

"Well there's my problem, see. I don't know what it is you want me to do."

"You are doing it."

"Just the same, don't you think it'd be a good idea to let me in on the secret? Maybe I could do it better and faster, tidier, if I know what it is."

"When the time is right, be assured you will be told all. In the meantime it is better for your own peace of mind that we proceed as we are proceeding."

"Will you verify what Julie told me just before you joined us? Is she indeed Luh-ill-ro-too?"

"She was, yes."

"But not now?"

"Not now. You are wondering about her awakening."

Bransen; the guy had never had a sense of humor that I could detect.

I would have liked to talk to Dalton again. I was a lot more curious now than before about the actual circumstances of that encounter in the canyon. Maybe the guy had a different angle on it now. But I had no good contacts at County and I knew that a casual inquiry would get me nowhere. So I brainstormed it and again went to the phone, called the records section at the hospital, and gave the girl a pitch. Deputy Dalton had left some personal effects in his room when he checked out. I wanted to send the stuff on to him, so I needed a home address and hopefully a phone number. A cheerful female clerk happily provided both, and felt good doing it. I felt good getting it, especially since the address was only about ten minutes away and on the route to LAX.

I reached Dalton's apartment complex a few minutes before eleven but then it took me another ten minutes to find the apartment in that sprawl.

It was obviously a bachelor pad, and the young deputy had company—two other guys—obviously cops also. They were drinking beer and watching a fight on television.

Dalton looked okay, relaxed, confident. I knew by the way he looked at me that I was familiar but he did not have me pegged. I knew also that I had to say the right thing at the right time or get the door slammed in my face.

So I introduced myself by name only and told him, "I need your help. I saw the same thing you saw in Malibu Canyon the other night. No one will believe me either."

He stared at me for a moment then threw the door wide

and beckoned me inside. It was a small apartment, and the TV fight was on low volume. The other guys heard my pitch at the door and they were giving me an interested inspection as I joined them.

Dalton introduced us. One was Sam and the other was John; I got no last names. Someone handed me a can of beer then they all sat down. I popped the top and took a taste as I took a chair off to the side. We sat there and watched the fight, with no conversation other than comments on the fighters. Everyone but me got up and peed between rounds, so it was a lot of traffic and no conversation to amount to anything. There was a knockout in the next round, though. Dalton turned the TV off and we all just sat there nursing our beers for a couple of minutes.

I had the drift of it. Misery loves company, everyone seems to think, so Dalton's buddies had come over to cheer him up. But misery is also contagious and I think the thing was working in that direction. It was a very sober group, beers notwithstanding.

Finally one of the other cops—John or Sam, I don't know—looked at me and said, "You saw it, eh?"

I said, "Yeah. Big as life. Damnedest thing I ever saw."

"Did you file a report?" the other buddy asked.

I said, "You kidding? Look at the way they're treating Grover. Who needs that?"

Dalton shot me an oblique gaze and quietly asked, "How'd you know where I live?"

I said, "I tracked you from the hospital."

He said, "Okay, I gotcha. What the hell is this? Are you a doctor or not?"

I said, "Not. Right now I'm a UFO investigator. I take

you for a very bright young cop and I know your story is true because I picked up the woman."

There followed a very long silence.

All eyes were on me.

John or Sam, whichever, broke the silence to ask me, "Exactly what is a UFO investigator?"

I replied, "If you're asking for credentials, forget it, I don't have any." I placed a business card on the coffee table. "I'm a private contractor. Right now, I am my only client. Look, I saw the saucer and I found the woman up above Pepperdine. She was blown clear out of her mind and knows nothing about what happened up there."

All three men were checking out my card, though none touched it.

I went on: "I'm just trying to put the thing together for my own satisfaction. I am not filing any useless reports or talking to any assholes in government. But I'm like Grover. I saw it and I can't forget it. So I thought maybe we could compare notes."

Dalton picked up the card and handed it back to me. "I already told everything I know," he said quietly.

I said, "Sure you did. But you don't see it in the papers, do you. The department will never release that report."

He lit a cigarette and stared at me across the glowing tip. "Who's the woman?"

"I can't tell you that."

"Then get your ass out of here."

I said, "It's confidential and she'll deny it. I'll deny it, too, if I'm ever asked. So it's strictly between us. The woman is Penny Laker."

That drew a snicker, a grin, and a wide-eyed look.

The wide eyes were on Deputy Dalton.

I saw a truth dawning in that look, a remembrance, a recognition. "Jesus," he whispered. "I knew she was familiar, but it was all so..."

I told him, "I chanced upon her while you were chasing the saucer. Her mind was blown, temporarily. I naturally assumed that she'd had an encounter with the saucer, maybe she'd been abducted and then set free. She fought me like crazy at first. But now I'm wondering if I had it right. I can't give you the details because I don't have any details, but it just doesn't feel right, now, that she was running from the saucer. I think she was running from something or someone else. Since you were in the area ahead of me, I thought maybe you saw something I didn't."

"Like what?"

"Like another vehicle, another person, anything."

"There was a car," the cop said slowly. "Making a U-turn in the Pepperdine drive. Fancy. Like a Rolls."

I let out my breath and asked, "Or a Bentley?"

Dalton flashed his eyes at me and replied, "Could be, yeah."

I said, "Thanks," and handed my card back to him.

He took it, dropped it in his shirt pocket, asked me, "Does Miss Laker drive a Bentley?"

I told him, "I understand that Miss Laker doesn't drive, period. But there's a Bentley in the family."

He said, "I see."

I said, "Well don't go looking for it. It's in Argentina."

"What does that mean?"

"I'm not sure I know what it means," I lied. "It was parked in front of my house a short while before your incident. I live in Malibu, on the beach. Miss Laker's husband came to see me about a personal problem. The last I saw of that Bentley it was headed south on Pacific Coast Highway and a saucer was following it."

I had the full attention of the house, now. Whatever else, these guys were cops and their cop instincts were at full extension. John or Sam quietly asked, "The same saucer?"

"It was the only saucer I saw that night," I replied, not yet ready to spill all of my guts. "I didn't see Grover's saucer—I mean, not in the same area. But his saucer sounds exactly like my saucer."

"Twelve to fifteen feet in diameter," Dalton said quietly.

"I called it at twelve feet," I told him. "That's a ballpark guess."

"Same ballpark," he said, smiling at me for the first time.

"Same ball, probably," I replied, smiling back.

"What was that bit about Argentina?"

"Miss Laker's husband is also her business manager. His name is Ted Bransen. We're not exactly friends because I'm more choosy than that but I've known him for several years. His wife, too. I told you that Bransen came to my house that night on a business matter, something to do with his wife. He wanted me to counsel her, some career matter. I agreed to discuss the problem with him over lunch the next day. Instead he called me from Buenos Aires in a panic. Claims he started off for his office that morning and found himself in Buenos Aires eight hours later, still in his Bentley and with no memory of those eight hours."

The cops exchanged looks with each other.

I got up and went to the door.

Dalton came over and shook my hand. "Thanks for the information, Mr. Ford," he said soberly.

I shrugged and replied, "For what it's worth, sure. Thanks for yours."

"For what it's worth," he said with a grim smile.

It was worth a hell of a lot to me.

I just needed to decide, now, what it all meant. And maybe I needed to reach that decision before I reached LAX.

CHAPTER TWENTY-SIX

Mission Possible

The flight was right on time and Bransen was one of the first passengers off. Things were sort of quiet at LAX that time of night so I had not been worried about missing him. Just the same, I was glad to see him coming off the ramp and I was positioned to snare him as soon as he stepped into the terminal.

I put an arm on the guy before he actually saw me, and it really startled him. I could see the whites of his eyes as they rolled toward me and he gave a little involuntary gasp and stiffened as though to pull away from my grasp, but he recovered quickly in recognition and tried to laugh it away but it was more like a dry rattle in a throat constricted by terror, not humor.

I pulled him out of the stream of traffic and directed him toward the escalator as I told him how I'd volunteered to make the pickup, but the guy was damned near a basket case. He didn't even inquire about Penny and apparently had no interest in local happenings during his absence. He had no baggage so we went straight across to the parking garage and we were on our way and moving in thin traffic just minutes later.

Only then did Bransen seem to relax a little and make a stab at conversation. "Thanks for, uh, your help down there."

I said, "Sure."

"I could have been tied up for days trying to straighten that mess out by myself."

I grinned at him and told him, "Just be glad you're not locked up."

"Right," he said, "or in a straitjacket. So I owe you. Remember that when you're making out your bill."

"There's no bill, Ted," I replied. "But I would like to know what the hell is going on."

"Tell me about it," he growled.

"Well let's tell each other," I suggested.

"I already told you all I know about this craziness. I guess you're the expert, so maybe you better tell me."

I said, "Okay. I think you're maybe married to an alien."

"What do you mean?"

"I don't mean a European immigrant, pal."

"Well that's crazy."

"Sure it's crazy, but it's a crazy time. I'll give you some more crazy. A flying saucer followed you away from my house the other night. A little while later I think I was directed into the hills above Pepperdine where I discovered your wife staggering naked along the highway. At that same time, a sheriff's deputy was chasing a low-flying saucer through the canyon. What do you make of that?"

Bransen's eyes were getting a bit wild again but I could also feel the defenses rising as he replied, "Do a treatment on that and I'll sell it to Spielberg. What do you mean you were *directed?*"

"Telepathically."

"Uh-huh. I thought that's what you meant. Look, I don't buy that stuff, Ford."

"But you do buy your wife wandering a lonely highway in the middle of the night, naked and defenseless."

"I don't get you."

"I got you, though, pal. You weren't surprised to hear about that because you already knew about it. So tell me: why did you drug your wife and turn her out of your car up there in the wilds?"

"You're out of your goddamn mind! What is this? Stop the goddamn car! I'm not going to ride with a maniac!"

I ignored all that. "And what were you setting me up for?—an alibi in advance?—the poor worried husband consulting a psychic quack as the only route to his wife's dementia?"

"Look who's talking about setups! Your Mission Impossible stunt was damned neat, Ford, damned near had me convinced!"

I told him, "You've been too close to the business too long, Ted. All of life is just another hackneyed script to you, isn't it, embellished with special effects and razzle-dazzle. Well you've run into a real one now, my friend, and you're fucking around with some real power. You'll know what I mean when you get home and find the new swimming pool and a pod of dolphins in your backyard."

He yelled, "Stop the goddamn car!"

"You don't really want me to do that," I replied mildly,

but I pulled to the curb anyway. We had reached that section of Century Boulevard just short of the freeway, where the airport hotels were clustered, and I knew what the guy was thinking; it was a good spot to bail out.

Or so he thought.

He opened the door and put one leg outside then froze, looked into the sky directly above the car, pulled his leg back inside, and gently closed the door.

"Let's go," he muttered.

"You sure?"

"Let's go, let's go."

So we went on.

With a twelve-foot saucer tracking us from about two hundred feet up.

The guy was already at the breaking point. It took very little persuasion to move him on into total surrender and docile cooperation. I feel that he came entirely clean with me, if you discount the normal and even understandable residual of self-serving alibis and rationalizations, which are entirely transparent anyway.

And it was a hackneyed script, yeah—the ancient human story retold through all the ages, revolving on greed and selfishness and the lust for survival in a competitive world.

"Look, I worked for that money, too. I mean I humbled myself and humiliated myself and kissed every ass in town to get her the very best deal every time. She didn't care. She never cared about any of it. The money meant nothing to her. She gave it away faster than I could claw it together for her.

"Well, hey, it's a community-property state—right?

We file joint returns—right? Half of it was mine, and I was just trying to protect what was mine."

I said, "Sure."

"Right." He leaned forward to peer up through the top of the windshield, flinched, and quickly withdrew with his head pressed against the backrest. "Anyway I started writing the contracts with deferred payments. We have about ten mil outstanding now. I was trying to protect it for her too, Ford. I figured someday she'll come to her senses and realize the value of a dollar. I didn't want her to be broke when that happened."

"'Course not."

"Right. Look, *I* knew she was not responsible. But it can be tricky as hell trying to convince a judge that it's true. I didn't want to hurt her."

"No way."

"No way is right. I was just trying to protect her, in her own interests, in both our interests. Isn't that a husband's obligation?"

"Sure it is."

"That's the way I saw it."

"So you just did a script for her."

"Right. That's the way to look at it. She's so damned dingy, Ford. I just needed to document it."

"Well... and maybe set the stage a little. A few props."

"Props, right. You have to have evidence when you go to the judge."

"Even if you have to manufacture some."

"Right, in her best interests."

"Uh-huh. So when you took her up into the Malibu hills...?"

"Well it was just . . . I mean, it was a setup, sure, but I didn't see that I was endangering her. I mean, the college was right there. I figured she'd wander in there and some kids would find her and . . ."

"But you didn't stick around to make sure it turned out that way. You didn't figure her to stagger along the road, instead, and try to flag down passing cars stark naked."

"'Course not."

"And you couldn't be expected to know about her alien past, so how could you know how the drug would affect her?"

"That's right."

"You couldn't know that she would run from her own guardians."

"Did she?"

"I think so. It's the only logic I can draw. Whatever you gave her, it really screwed her up."

"It was just a little acid."

"You never know what that stuff will do. Even on a human."

He shivered. "Well she *is* human."

I said, "Maybe not."

"I know damn well she's human. Shared her bed for years. Don't tell me she's not human."

I shrugged. "Well, mammalian at least."

"What are these things? What are they doing here? What do they want?"

"The saucers?"

He peered into the sky again. "Yeah."

I told him, "I don't know what the hell they are, Ted. I don't know why they're here and I don't know what they want. But they are here. So it must be for something important. And you can bet your ass they'll get whatever it is they want."

"I keep thinking I'll wake up," Bransen replied weakly.

"I guess that's what everybody thinks," I said.

Sure. I suppose I kept expecting to wake up any minute, myself. But even my dreams knew better.

CHAPTER TWENTY-SEVEN

Night of the Dolphin

In any other context, Ted Bransen's vicious little crimes against his wife would have warranted a story all their own. In the context given, they are hardly worthy of a footnote—because this is not a story of petty human greed and treachery but one of truly cosmic significance.

I do believe, you see, that these beings in their marvelous flying machines are our gods and angels of all the world's myths and legends and holy scripts. They have left their imprints and their promises on every genetic tracing upon the planet earth, within every culture and society and race of man, and they are part of us today as always in the past—because they are us in their roots and we are them in our destiny.

I mentioned earlier the technological advances possible in a mere two hundred years of steady progress. Consider then if you will that these beings were intergalactic travelers when the first man appeared upon the earth, perhaps a million years ago. Virtually the entire story of mankind thus far has been concerned with the need to dominate his environment; only when that was largely achieved could this upstart species begin to reach beyond its own immediate needs, and only in the present century has that reach become directed toward other worlds.

The human race has not yet been born into cosmos.

We have become impregnated with the idea and the possibility, yes, but our position in a cosmic society is still that of a remote aboriginal tribe buried in its own ignorance, frightened and suspicious of the missionaries who come from other worlds to encourage us in our reach. Our medicine men and shamans jealously guard their own puny power and hurl their superstitions into our midst whenever the missionaries are sighted, ridiculing and tarring and banishing all who would notice them. But the missionaries do keep coming, and the impressions continue to be made, and mankind does keep inching toward that launch into the cosmic community.

I believe that is the whole story of the flying saucers, whether they be no more than psychic images displayed for our edification or truly chariots of fire piloted by god-like beings who think of us as their future as we think of our own children as ours.

They come to us from time to time, when the need is there or when the opportunity for growth is there—to teach, to inspire, to guide, or to give us a kick in the pants when that is needed.

I believe that they are among us now in greater numbers and in growing interest because of our own intense development over the past sixty years. This could be a critical time for the planet called earth, a time for huge decisions and planetary commitments beyond anything yet dreamt by the human mind, and it could decide the fate of our species.

I believe all this because I believe that Donovan told it to me. Of course I am not one hundred percent certain that Donovan even exists except in my own mind, because I know that my mind creates its own reality. But if I think, therefore I am, then I am, therefore Donovan is—and the one thing encompasses the other, doesn't it.

But I have gotten ahead of my story.

Let's go back to Brentwood, as I think it existed on that third night of the California UFO flap... the night of the dolphins.

I remember an incident from my Navy days when I was sailing a small sloop with a friend on Chesapeake Bay. I'd gone below to get a thermos of coffee, and when I poked my head back on deck we were passing directly under the bow of the U.S.S. *Nimitz*, one of our nuclear aircraft carriers which are the largest combat vessels afloat. I had never before looked at one from that particular point of view, but it was a view I would never forget. That ship is over a thousand feet long. It displaces close to a hundred thousand tons in full combat load. It carries three thousand men in the ship's company and another twenty-six hundred in the air wing. It is also a mobile base for ninety combat aircraft.

Impressive as all that is, I give it only as an unimpressive comparison to the thing I found hovering above Brentwood at about one-thirty that morning.

Donovan later told me that they could take the *Nimitz* on board if they so desired.

It is mind-boggling just to see something like that

hanging there in the sky with no apparent support, no motion, and in absolute silence.

You get the feeling that it's just not possible; nothing that big could even get off the ground let alone hang there like that.

We spotted the thing when we were about two minutes away from the house. It was no more than a hundred feet off the ground but it was showing no lights and I first took it to be a low cloud. In fact my mind leaped from that identification to the "fog" of the night before and I was playing with that idea when the various features began materializing as we drew closer, and I knew it was neither fog nor cloud but a vessel looming up as the *Nimitz* had done on Chesapeake Bay years earlier.

It was a stunning sight and both I and my passenger were appropriately stunned by it.

This was no flying saucer, understand, in the same sense that the U.S.S. *Nimitz* is not a Phantom jet.

And of course you can rationalize a flying saucer until it disappears as swamp gas or a weather balloon, but no way can you con the mind into accepting something like this as anything but what it is: a huge physical mass stationary in the sky.

Bransen gasped, "What th' hell *is* that thing?"

I muttered, "More to the point, why is it hovering above your house?"

I had brought the Maserati to a halt atop a small knoll about a thousand yards from the house. We had a perfect profile view of the thing, with its lower edge just slightly higher than we were. Using the house as a scale, I guessed the hull area at several hundred feet deep and I could discern vague details of a superstructure above that. Bransen's house was dwarfed beneath the thing.

I took my foot off the brake and eased ahead.

"Where the hell are you going?" Bransen cried.

I said, "They know we're here, pal. May as well take it all the way."

He threw his door open and flung himself through it. We were moving no faster than five miles per hour so I was not all that concerned about him bailing out, and in fact I saw it only with my peripheral vision because all my attention was directed straight ahead, but I did become a bit puzzled when it dawned on me that Bransen was remaining in my peripheral vision even though the car was definitely moving forward. So I shot a quick glance that way and saw the guy standing in midair beside the car. Only then did I realize that the car, too, was airborne and moving at the same slow rate of speed directly toward the floating city.

That is all I remember about that.

I was standing at the oval window beside Donovan as he monitored the operations below. There was a great deal of activity down there and also in the airspace between house and ship. The entire area was brilliantly lighted, without shadows or relief of any kind. Small saucers were darting about, many of them, and I could see several on the ground behind the house.

I said to Donovan, "I don't want to try to tell you how to run your show, but this thing must be showing up on radar screens clear to the Kremlin. Isn't there some way to do this in a less conspicuous way?"

He gave me an indulgent smile as he replied, "Who

would believe it?" Then he laughed and said, "We are opaque to such energies only when we choose to be, so don't be concerned about the radars."

"Okay. But they can probably see your lights at LAX. Come on, Donovan, this isn't the wilds of New Mexico; it's Southern California. You can't pull an operation like this without terrorizing millions of people."

"Then where are the interceptors?" he asked humorously. "Relax, my brother. We are seen when we choose to be seen, and then only."

I said, "Then you're dammit not real. You are psychological phenomena."

He chuckled. "What is not? If you are interacting with psychological phenomena, then are you inside or outside the phenomena?"

I tried to focus on the question but the attempt dizzied me. Everything went black for a moment and I said, "Dammit, Donovan."

With no apparent loss of continuity, then, I found myself on the ground beneath the ship and I was gazing up at it with awe and a trembly kind of excitement. The saucers were still flitting about and I could see now that they were flying in and out of a huge bay on the underside of the big carrier. But the mental comparative image I got was not that of a Navy carrier launching and receiving aircraft but of a colony of bees buzzing around their hive, with no apparent logic to their movements.

There was much activity all around me on the ground, also. Many strange buglike "things" were scuttling about the pool, both in and out of the water. The human mind is not a simple plastic web, you know, it is not like a lens or a mirror that simply seizes what is out there; it is a highly complicated quantum quality that is constantly constructing and reshaping itself from billions of sense receptors all firing individual messages—so don't ask me to give you a calm and rational account of what was going on there. I did not know what was going on there because my mind did not know how to assimilate the evidence from the sense receptors. There simply was no model from my reality world which could serve the understanding. So the mind shorts out, in a sense. You either pass out or you pass over into a more limited scan of what is there, seeking shapes and forms that are more assimilable and perhaps more malleable.

So I do not know exactly what I was seeing there. I know only what I was experiencing, and that was buglike objects running around like crazy all over the place while small flying discs darted about in their midst.

The only comforting thing I "saw" in all that was a vision or an image of Penny Laker. She wore a silver bodysuit and she was in the pool between two dolphins, her arms around them as they swam leisurely along the surface of the water.

Then Julie joined me and gave me a casual hug from the side as we watched Penny with her dolphins. I felt loved and loving but did not know why until Julie wiped a tear from her cheek and said to me, "Now *that* is love."

And I knew that it really was.

CHAPTER TWENTY-EIGHT

The Residual

I am reasonably confident that most of what I have told you to this point is more or less true. From this point forward, however, I am not sure that any of it is true, or complete, or valid in any sense.

What I have here now, I think, is like a residual of experience from which perhaps my own mind has drawn certain conclusions—yet at the same moment I can hear Donovan's voice narrating the story as I struggle to record it in a language that you and I can understand, so perhaps there is more here than any of us are able to comprehend at the moment.

It comes to me that Donovan's people are extremely ancient. I have a sensing here of time beyond time, or time beyond any meaning of time. Earth scientists now place the birth of the universe at some ten to twenty billion years ago. Certainly that is time beyond meaning for most of us since it is at least twice the age of our own solar system, and the time of life itself on earth, even microscopic life, is again about half the age of our planet.

Yet I have images in my mind of a time when people like me, Donovan's people, watched with interest the birth of this solar system and its subsequent slow development as a new home for life in the universe, a development that required more than two billion years of processing before a life environment was achieved.

And if other images are valid, then there is no need to wonder about man's wanderlust because we were born to it as a result of an incredible odyssey that predates all our concepts of time itself and lies before us still as an infinite spiral without a beginning and without an end. For Donovan's people—and we too are those people—are older than time and concepts of time.

That means also, of course, that we are older than space-time matter itself, for time is the measure of that matter.

Older than time, we are nevertheless bound to time by our interactions with matter and bound to the space-time universe by our involvement with life and its narrow band of environmental interactions. No single star can support our reach because our reach is eternal and the stars are not. Therefore the odyssey, and the constant search for home in an evolving and temporal universe.

As the sensing of universal time infiltrates my model of reality, I find Donovan's people arriving on this planet the first time as a scouting expedition only.

They found a breathable atmosphere and a hospitable ecosystem, an advanced stage of organic evolution and a profusion of higher life-forms, with the most successful forms adapted to the marine environment.

This advance party established a base for scientific studies and performed various genetic experiments on several similar lines of the higher land-dwelling animals.

They also studied marine species and concluded that the earth was a "water planet" and favored the evolution of life within the seas.

It was much later when the first colonists arrived, perhaps one or two million years later, and they found a far different planet than the one cataloged during the earlier visitation.

Various solar dynamics and planetary processes had combined to raise extensive new landmasses from the seas and the climate was generally inhospitable except for a narrow band along the equatorial bulge.

Also a totally new species had appeared among the land-dwelling animals, and this new species was unsettlingly similar to themselves.

They called this new development *A'd'um* and genetically traced its origins to the experiments conducted by the original survey team.

Even more unsettling was the discovery that some 100,000 A'd'ums were scattered in small social groups throughout the land areas of the equatorial bulge.

This presented a moral dilemma to the settlers, who were in far smaller numbers and with a precarious toehold on the planet.

They could not possibly take on responsibilities for these primitive creatures, yet they felt responsible by virtue of the genetic endowment from them that lifted A'd'um definitely out of the unrealized pool of planetary life into the exalted self-knowing realm of universal intelligence.

Remember that these D'Ahnov'e'ns were a very ancient race even before our solar system was born. They possessed an almost godlike moral sense and an entirely responsible stance regarding the expansion of intelligent life in the universe.

I have earlier picturesquely referred to them as "missionaries" but that is hardly an adequate term to convey their sense of oneness with the creative principle.

Already they had come to think of themselves as God's partners and helpers in the spatial dimensions of time; perhaps they even regarded themselves as coexistent with the creative principle, and maybe they are.

But there was no practical way to resolve the dilemma posed by the appearance of A'd'um. Thus a "tension" was forged between the two similar groups on earth, a relationship which modern mystics would characterize as "karmic." They were bound together not only by shared genetic structures but equally by moral responsibility.

The D'Ahnov'e'ns could not directly manipulate A'd'um's world but they could not turn their backs on them either. Isolation was the only solution—apparent isolation, anyway, from A'd'um's point of view—with D'Ahnov'e'n remaining aloof yet cognizant and remotely supportive, A'd'um largely unaware of the other's existence except in startling moments of accidental confrontation.

Thus developed the two families of D'Ahnov'e'n side by side on planet earth, separated more by time and circumstance than anything else, and thus they all prospered for thousands of years.

But then came another time of solar upheaval and another crushing moral dilemma.

The "gods" gave up their planet, leaving A'd'um behind to ride out the convulsive cataclysms of a world gone mad, where oceans invaded the continents and the continents exploded into new configurations invading the heavens, and the seas boiled.

All to his credit, A'd'um hung on.

To his everlasting shame and karmic debt, D'Ahnov'e'n left him to that chaos and to that hell. Together, however—and following the same principle of isolation that held before—they have been building a new heaven ever since.

Time was coming into sync.

D'Ahnov'e'n's time was becoming A'd'um's time.

Time to time and hand in hand, the way was being prepared for them to go forward together into cosmos.

I think that is all true.

I hope that it is.

The alternative, I fear, is the night of the dolphin.

CHAPTER TWENTY-NINE

Future Perfect

There were saucers of every size and description parked in the big vehicle bay or flight deck or whatever, several as large as fifty feet in diameter—which Donovan identified as "star craft"—and others no larger than a garbage can cover. I asked him about the tiny ones and he told me that they were "sensor scouts." He did not elaborate and it did not seem appropriate to question further because we'd reached the far end of the catwalk and he was guiding me into this other large chamber.

In there, the lighting was soft like twilight and there was a hum in the air, not like machinery but like hundreds of voices doing a one-note mantra. Pictures were flickering on the walls in about fifty different patches and there seemed to be a hundred or so people intently engrossed at a variety of consolelike devices.

"Operations Control," Donovan explained as we crossed overhead.

"You run a tight ship," I observed.

"Oh we must," he assured me.

Then we went up a circular stairway and into paradise. I know no other word fitting to describe this place. It was like a beautiful park with low rolling hills, grass and trees and flowers, streams and small waterfalls. We'd come up almost into the center of it, yet it was difficult to see to the end of it in any direction. Obviously it took up one entire level of this floating city. And it was not a static scene. People were scattered throughout—playing, talking, reading, whatever people do anywhere to relax, and I saw children too. The formfitting bodysuit seemed to be standard but there were many different colors and even some in multicolors.

I said to Donovan, "This is very nice."

"The swimming pools are over there," he said, pointing. "There are game courts at the peripheries." He smiled at me. "We have concerts under the stars in the evenings. They are very popular. Of course there are other diversions possible in the private quarters but we do encourage community to every practical extent."

I was looking about, soaking up the delightful atmosphere, as I commented, "This could be any beautiful spot on earth."

He said, "Or on any earth. Environments are very important, Ashton. Especially on long sojourns. And we cannot encourage our people to sample alien habitats."

"Meaning no shore leave," I said.

"Nothing is forbidden," he corrected me.

"You've come a long way, baby," I told him.

"To live in harmony is the greatest joy," he told me, the only platitude he ever gave me, and this one came not as a platitude but as an explanation.

* * *

The Maserati was on a little revolving platform and a group of people were standing around admiring it, like in an automobile showroom, while another guy opened and closed the doors, the hood, and the engine compartment. He also honked the horn a couple of times and started the engine, shifted forward and reverse and crept along for a few inches in each direction, operated the headlights and the windshield wipers. During all this, the other people are smiling and nodding their heads and making comments back and forth.

I asked Donovan, "Would you please ask the guy to be careful with the Maserati? She is my greatest treasure and truest love."

He chuckled and replied, "Don't worry about your car, Ashton. It is in the very best of hands. But you really should examine your attitudes there, my friend. A machine is not worthy of love and it is the most perishable of treasures."

"Well that one is worthy of my love," I argued, "and I'm going to be *buried* in it, so we'll perish together."

Donovan just laughed.

But I noticed that his people were really digging the car.

We were standing at the oval window and I saw two dolphins fly by. They looked unconscious to me. I asked Donovan, "Are they okay?"

"They're fine," he assured me. "They'll be home before they know it and they won't remember a thing."

"Just how intelligent are these dolphins?" I asked him.

He said, "Depends on where you're measuring from. Also there are differences between individuals, the same as any species. These fellows will never build star cruisers. But they'll never need to do so, either. The dolphins, Ashton, should be your teachers when it comes to the art of loving relationships."

I asked him, "What are you doing with them? What's this all about?"

"We are discharging a debt, Ashton."

"What kind of debt?"

"Well, we stole their planet, didn't we."

I said, "Did we?"

"Of course. They were the soul of the planet, my brother. We nudged them aside and substituted our own. In ignorance, of course, but... ah, well. This will help."

"What will help?"

"Well, you—we corrupted their environment. Looted and pillaged it, didn't we. The ecology of the entire planet has been altered. These fellows were not designed to cope with the environmental side effects of rampant technology. They would never survive it, just as we would not if confined to a single planet."

"I've seen those fellows on another planet," I reminded him.

"Oh that wasn't a planet," Donovan replied.

"Then what was it? You told me it was real."

"Real enough, yes. And entirely real for them. It is a world they built for themselves, Ashton."

I caught my breath in a sudden insight. "Built by their minds!"

"Yes. So what is technology, eh?"

I couldn't let it go that easy, though. I said, "Some Indian tribes have a happy hunting ground, a reverie land and what have you, which they believe they can visit. The dolphins . . . ?"

"Yes," Donovan replied, "and others in their family, as well. What you call the killer whale has evolved a beautiful dreamland which they visit annually in large groups from a small bay in Canada. But of course all the dreamlands will be lost if the planet is lost. Earth is but a base, you see, for all the dreamlands that arise from it. So it is much more than a mere planet in space and time."

I felt absolutely staggered by the concept.

I told Donovan, "Okay. Now maybe I know who the devil is."

"It is us," he said simply.

"We can change it," I decided.

"We are changing it," Donovan told me.

"What are you doing to the dolphins?"

"Preparing them."

"For what?"

"To inherit the earth."

"After?"

"After his cousins render it unfit for their own further habitation. They will abandon it then, as all the others. We are introducing new strains of genetic components, Ashton. The dolphin will adapt and survive. So think of him as your successor."

"And what of us?" I asked quietly.

"I assumed that was obvious," he replied. "Look at me, Ashton. I am your future." He touched a plate on the wall, and the scene through the oval window became a long shot of the floating city as viewed from far away. "And look at this. It is your future home."

I said, "I'm not sure I like it, Donovan."

"Pity," he said. "It has been your goal for eight hundred million years."

CHAPTER THIRTY

Time Out

Operation Dolphin was winding down. The shuttling of saucers back and forth across the airspace had given way to cleanup operations on the ground. Several small saucers were moving slowly about like vacuum cleaners, sucking up all the debris and the evidence of the night. I was seated in the lanai at the table with Penny and Julie. We just sat there, silent, watching the cleanup. Both women wore the characteristic silver bodysuit. I studied them for a moment, wondering, then I felt Donovan's mind on mine. I stood up and went to the corner of the lanai to peer up at the celestial city. Instantly then I found myself at the opposite end, peering back at myself on the ground.

Donovan stood beside me. He put an arm around me and squeezed me at the shoulder level. "Thank you, Ashton. You won't forget us, will you?"

"Fat chance," I said. "But thanks for what? I've done nothing."

"You've done more than you realize," he assured me. "But the thanks is for future favors as well."

I told him, "I have no idea what you're talking about. I know nothing of what I am supposed to do."

"As it should be. You will recognize it when it comes."

I asked him, "Are you taking the girls with you?"

"Oh no. Their work is here."

"For how long?"

"How does one measure the length of a life? Where does it begin and where does it end?"

I said, "Are you telling me they're here for life?"

He nodded. "For this life."

"I'm confused about this," I told him. "I would have sworn that both of those women were...different. Julie even spoke to me in some alien tongue while she was in trance. Now you seem to be saying..."

"Of course they are different, as each soul is unique and special. They came into this life pledged to a specific task. You would call them specialists, and they came to apply their specialty. At the proper time they were awakened. Granted, the awakening is sometimes confusing and even painful, especially if a period of retraining is deemed advisable, but—"

"You've had them in a training program?"

"Penelope, yes, because of the delicacy of the mission. Julie...well, not retraining but...Julie had never consolidated her role, let's put it that way. Therefore her awakening was particularly sluggish. I am telling you this, Ashton, only because I know you will take no offense at your role in her awakening."

I muttered, "That's what it was, eh? You needed someone to awaken the woman in her? Instead of what?—a dolphin?"

"I have told you there are many worlds, Ashton. There are also various dimensions and various stages of life. And there are harmonic realms. Now...your planet occupies a transfer realm, a vibrant of harmonics. Therefore there is much passage here, realm to realm. Have you not yet detected the very special dualism of qualities here?"

I said, "If you're talking about soul, or spirit...and that reminds me: what is this bit with the triangle and the pyramid?"

He smiled and again squeezed my shoulder. "Gave you something to think about, eh? The triangle is no more than the unity, Ashton, the statement in truth. In this your vibrant harmonic, the base leg of the triangle is beingness. The rising legs signify the projection and the return."

"Projection to where?"

"To God, of course."

I said, "Uh-huh. And the pyramid?"

"The promise."

"Promise of what?"

"Eternity. Have you understood nothing from me, my brother? Have I not told you of your many voyages upon the seas of time and of the timelessness of your quest? Why are you confused about your sisters when you and they are one? There are no alien languages, Ashton, there is but the projection and the return. Which role shall you project this time?–and which role shall return to project again? Your planet is a harmonic base, my friend, and your time here is but the base of the triangle."

I said, "This is confusing, Donovan. I get the feeling

you are talking about repeated lives in different bodies—and that's okay, I can think about that—but you've also been talking to me about a physical as opposed to a spiritual odyssey, and I'm having trouble separating the two."

"That is because they cannot be separated," he replied. "Stop trying to separate and begin the attempt to unify. After all, Ashton, it is all a single reality."

Suddenly I was on the ground again, peering up from the corner of the lanai. The floating city was not there but a twelve-foot saucer was. It wiggled at me, then winked out.

I muttered, "Okay," and went back to join the ladies at the table.

The dawn was breaking. Julie showed me a self-conscious little smile and poured coffee for me.

I said, "Well, it's been quite a night."

Penny told me, "You are welcome to join us for any sunrise, Ashton. It is always a very special moment, isn't it."

I looked at her and then at Julie and replied, "Yes, especially after a very special night."

Penny laughed and said, "Well I guess that's one way of looking at it. But I always think of sunrise as the beginning of a very special day."

I lowered my eyes to my coffee and replied, "For special people, yeah."

The vibes there were really weird. I had the god-awful feeling that neither of these ladies had been where I had been for the past few hours.

Almost as though to dispute that impression, though, Penny put a hand on my arm and said, "Thank you again, darling, for taking such good care of me last night. And I promise I will never do such a foolish thing again. Poor Ted. I cannot imagine how he must have felt when I bolted away from him like that." She showed me the patented Laker smile. "Well, all's well that ends well. Thanks to you, my love."

Now I felt even weirder. *Last* night? Had she lost the entire experience?

Julie showed me another of those embarrassed smiles and told Penny, "Ashton is interested in our dolphin watches. He's agreed to join us at Zuma next week."

I had?

"Well Ashton would be perfect for this!" Penny declared excitedly. "I'll bet he would make an excellent channel."

Channel? She meant medium.

I smiled secretly and told her, "I think I might have spoken with a dolphin once, maybe several of them."

Julie said, "Then maybe you could channel Ambudala."

I looked away and muttered, "Maybe I could."

"Dee Townsend receives him, but sort of erratically."

I was watching the sunrise as I asked, "Who is Ambudala?"

"Dee says he is a dolphin guide and teacher, a great master."

"In dolphin heaven," I decided.

"I guess so."

That is where we were when Bransen swept in, all bright-eyed and gung-ho and who would've dreamed it was him. He grabbed my hand and wrung it out, dropped kisses on the ladies, grabbed some coffee and walked out to look at the pool, came back with dancing eyes. "Fabulous job!" he said to Penny. "I wouldn't have believed they could put it in that quick! And not a clod of dirt anywhere! Who's the contractor?"

Penny told him, "Ashton brought him to us."

I looked at Bransen, thought *Oh well,* and told him, "Guy named Donovan. Specializes in, uh, unusual developments."

Bransen told his wife, "Keep that in mind. Maybe we can use him again. Listen, I bring back great news. This university down in Argentina is abandoning their marine research program. They have this great facility on a small offshore island with tanks, pens, the whole works in a strictly natural environment—absolutely the best for studying marine life. They'll lease the whole works on excellent terms. I took the liberty, Penny, of signing it on while I was there." He withdrew a document from his coat pocket and handed it to his wife.

I casually inquired, "When was this, Ted?"

He said, as though replying to the obvious, "Yesterday. You know? Buenos Aires?"

I said, "Oh, that yesterday."

He laughed and punched my arm. "Listen," he told me, "you're just the guy we need to round up the celebrities for next month's march."

I said, "Which march is that?"

"The nuclear protest, dummy. Nukes? Nevada? Underground tests?"

I said, "Oh, that march."

Well, that's the way it was going.

I figured what the hell and sat there and listened to about twenty minutes of the rebirth of Ted Bransen, then

Julie walked me to the carport and kissed me tenderly and we agreed to keep in touch.

The Maserati was sitting there cheek to jowl with Bransen's Bentley.

I winked at Julie and she winked back as I climbed into the Maserati, wondering if any of it had actually happened. Certainly *something* warm had happened with Julie . . . but what?

I eased away from there in a slow withdrawal, my gaze wandering repeatedly into the heavens. Then as I topped the little knoll where Bransen and I had paused earlier that morning, I spotted Grover Dalton.

He wore Levi's and a windbreaker and binoculars, and he was seated on the roof of his car with legs crossed and a thermos of coffee between them.

I halted beside him and asked, "Did you see it?"

He said, without looking at me, "Yeah, I saw it. Is it all over?"

"For this time, yeah, I think so," I told him. "May as well pack it in and take it home."

"Thanks," he said, "guess I'll give it a while longer. Got nothing else to do."

I knew the feeling.

I parked the Maserati and climbed up there with him. We shared the coffee and some small talk and waited together for possibly one last look.

They could have forgotten something.

What the hell, they *could* come back.

But of course they did not, not that time. They only come from time to time. They are older than time, you see, and they ride time like a steed throughout the universe.

What is time, anyway? If time is meaningless, then both past and future are mere abstracts, and forever is now.

And reality is a golden triangle.

Suggested Reading

Blum, Ralph with Judy Blum. *Beyond Earth: Man's Contact With UFOs*. New York: Bantam Books, 1974.

Downing, Barry H. *The Bible and Flying Saucers*. New York: J.B. Lippincott, 1968/Avon Books, 1970.

Fuller, John G. *The Interrupted Journey*. New York: The Dial Press, 1966.

Hynek, J. Allen. *The UFO Experience, A Scientific Inquiry*. New York: Henry Regnery, 1972/Ballantine Books, 1974.

Strieber, Whitley. *Communion*. New York: Beech Tree/William Morrow, 1987.

Tomas, Andrew. *We Are Not the First*. New York: G.P. Putnam's Sons, 1971/Bantam Books, 1973.

Le Poer Trench, Brinsley. *The Sky People*. London: Neville Spearman, 1965/New York: Award Books, 1970.